MOVIES IN MY HEAD

BY OTEP SHAMAYA

MOVIES IN MY HEAD

BY OTEP SHAMAYA

Centaurs Breed Publishing

Ω

Cover design by Trashbag Ghost
www.trashbagghost.com

MOVIES IN MY HEAD

BY OTEP SHAMAYA

Centaurs Breed Publishing

For information about this publication contact: **girlgoesgrrr@gmail.com**

For my muse, my guide, my rock, my beloved Mother. Thank you for always believing in me and for putting this fire inside my mind.

Table of Contents

PINE BOX JAKE

He looked off to the horizon. The long rays of the setting sun crowned the mountains with golden fire. He soaked it in as if it was the last time he'd ever see such a marvelous sight. A breeze drifted in. It lifted leaves from the trees, smelled of campfires and coffee, and carried a soft thrum from mysterious places.

Pinebox Jake stayed still for a spell, clinging to a rock like a possum on its mama's back, catching his breath and steadying himself from the fall. A damn funny sight for a man his size and disposition.

Hanging on and hanging tight, he half expected to see a roaring fountain of hellfire ripping upwards as the heavy gates of Hades unsealed to receive him. But it was nothing but loam and tunnel and stifling lightless black.

(the name…)

He tried wriggling up that slight bit of rock, his boots kicking like catfish on a line, going nowhere fast.

This was bad, he thought. Not as bad as killing his good-for-nothing pap with a shovel. Damn near cut his head clean off. Not as bad as being sent to that orphanage and killing that pederast preacher. Not as bad as shooting that dumbass in the back who tried kidnapping his younger sister. Or hiding out in the wild for a season, feuding with Injun slavers and whisky-soaked peckerwood fur trappers. Not as bad as half starving to death that lonely winter, eating rats and boiled tree bark. Not as bad as all that. But this was pretty bad.

"Slow and steady."

That's what he told them dumbasses as they lowered him – like a spider – down a rescue hole so small his shoulders barely fit through. Asses so dumb they couldn't pour piss from a boot with instructions on the heel.

(think of something else ...anything else)

He told them greenhorn dumbasses to tether him to a hoist, but they wouldn't listen. He told them to get an extra length of cable, but they wouldn't listen. Instead, they wrapped a rope around his waist and held the other end like they was playing tug-of-war. At least they let that Welsh dumbass tie the knot. He used to be a sailor. But then the ground began to quake and them dumbasses dropped the rope, leaving him to snatch whatever bit of rock he slammed into.

He grumbled something and spit. Then fired off a blistering array of profanity that would've made Satan himself blush. He let loose on all the rotten bastards and puddle-sucking dumbasses whose dastardly deeds had provoked and set forth the inevitable calamities that compelled him down into that awful fortress of rock. Deep and dreadful. Unimaginable darkness. He cursed the earth, the heavens, and all the dark devils of the godless black.

(think of ...)

His grip, much like the world above, was slipping away.

(anything but ...)

In an instant he was gone, tumbling end over end into nothingness. He was surprised at how quiet it was. He didn't holler or make even the slightest sound.

He just fell.

But the rope must've snagged on an outcropping or maybe them dumbasses up top managed to grab hold of it because he came to a quick and breathless halt.

So there he hung, suspended like a pendulum over the vacant innards of the earth, imbued with a queer optimism, looking this way and that for a causeway or an egress. Just...swinging. The rope moaned with the weight of him.

(...the name)

He adjusted his headlamp and some trick of the light animated his shadow. From a distance, his head was a little yellow moon swaying in the inky jaws of emptiness. But it was a transient stand. For as quick as it came, it ended just the same.

The rope unwound from around his waist and he rejoined the empty air, dropping down that jagged shaft without making a single sound.

He fell boots-first until the tunnel bottlenecked and he hit rock bottom. He was flat on his ass, face first against a wall of rock, wedged in a funnel. His boots dangled into the infinite empty like a child on a swing. A damn funny sight for a man his size and disposition.

(think of something else…)

There was rock in front of him and behind. Surrounding him like a well. It went up as high as he could see and funneled into a deep chasm just below his boots.

His mind ached at the thought that a blasted rescue team might be needed to rescue him from his own blasted rescue tunnel. He tried to tell them dumbass muckers that their calculations were off, that no way, no how, would this salvage tunnel intersect with the main vein of that mine. "Seven times five isn't seventy-five, you dumbasses," he told them – but they wouldn't listen. They never listened. But he couldn't think about that now.

(…anything else)

Because then, as if in a dream, shapes came out of the dark, advancing on him like clouds of scalding volcanic smoke. Shapes that amplified and multiplied from disordered faces to a quivering mosaic of full-bodied phantoms. Shapes that made him fearful he'd slipped into that bedlamite break between this world and the next, a locus of nightmares and madness. But he couldn't think about that now.

(not now)

The fall had so thoroughly unhinged him, he had trouble deciphering if he was upside down or right side up. And it was so tight in that wedge he could barely breathe. He hunched up like a spider and tried lifting himself but couldn't manage it. His muscles felt like they'd come loose from the bones. And he ached. It felt like there were hundreds of fire ants stinging his lower parts. He must've busted up his knee 'cause it hurt like hell to bend. He looked right, then left, hoping for a miracle. He coughed and felt a cold sweat spread down his neck.

(not the name, don't think of the name…)

He coughed again and it felt like burning branches inside his lungs. Damn it all. Back in camp, nearly half of the men were quarantined in fever sheds, coughing up a lung. Deep and croaky, the old cough of pestilence. The same cough that had detonated from his chest a half dozen times since he'd been down here. But he couldn't think about that now.

(not now)

He stayed still, calming his nerves, when a giggle rolled to a chuckle and he burst into gut-busting laughter.

Pinebox.

He 'd gotten that name when he was just a boy, for all the men he'd buried as a gravedigger in the war.

Then the name just sort of stuck, for all the men he'd buried as hired muscle for the Purple Orchid brothel back in Kansas City. It was anything goes in that rotten place, but there was one thing he couldn't abide – dumbasses hurtin' them girls.

Now look at him. Buried inside a hill called Horse Head, haloed by dumbasses. His name had gotten him into some tight spots before, but this was ridiculous.

He choked back a laugh, wiped fever sweat on his sleeve, and looked up that long cylinder of rock, hoping for a spot of sunlight.

But for the narrow cone of light from his headlamp, it was a great pit of sightless black.

(not your name… OUR name …the name of the…)

Trapped in the depths of that ultima Thule – that is to say, beyond the known world – he regretted not snapping the necks of them twin shit-heels, the Loving brothers, when he had the chance – up there – where it was sunny, and the air was clean. He growled like a bear protecting his kill.

"Them dumbasses are pro'ly holed up like kings," he said in a thick West Virginia twang, "spread out like opium smokers, drunker'n skunks, buried between the long legs of some sweet honey pots."

He pushed back against the slabs and heaved in a mighty breath. Then, another notion passed over him, this time a vision of a snake trying to swallow an egg.

He had to get moving.

He slid a pick-hammer from his belt and tapped around the tunnel for any loose rocks. Even the slightest avalanche could be fatal. A bit of rock slipped past his boots into the funnel, and he listened. It was damned quiet. So quiet you could hear a fly pissing on cotton. He listened, but it never did strike bottom.

But there was something – knocking or scratching – no, it was a voice – ricocheting in the nebulous depths.

"Ye gods," he whispered. Someone had survived the collapse. He tried to call out – coughed – and tried again.

"Hello?" his raspy voice echoed into the abyss.

"Otis, is that you, nephew?"

He listened hard into the great watery silence, but there weren't no reply. His ribs hurt. Probably cracked one in the fall. Oh, damn it all. If he got out of this jam, he thought, first thing he was gonna do was march to his brother-in-law's tent and punch that luckless sumbitch right in the nose. It was his idea to come west. It was his idea to join up with the Loving Brothers Mining Company.

"Oh, it's easy money, he says. Day wages, he says. You just pluck silver right outta the land, he says. Whisky springs and cigarette trees, he says. Oil runs like a river down them hills, he says."

He spit.

"Sumbitch's agility at copious sayin's will be considerably fucking difficult with a mouthful of my fist." He sat back and exhaled. Clouds of breath billowed up in the flicker of his headlamp.

And it was then that he saw *something* – slithering – just outside his light: a dull shape, a tangle of black spider webs, pooling and coiling inward then spreading out again. Appearing and disappearing, here and there, like a flock of mad birds. At times, it weren't no bigger than a loaf of bread. In the next instant, it went on a hundred miles (or seemed to) without wanting to end. Then, there came a hissing and a chattering like rats in a nest. He felt a presence in the dark. Words that weren't his rose up.

"Blood for blood," it said. *"Signed in …in…in blood. Fresh blood, young flesh."*

He was covered in spiders.

It felt like it anyway.

"Hold strong now."

He raked his stubbly beard with a trembling hand. A strange odor filled the cavern. Old rot, moldy flowers. It reminded him of a funeral. But he couldn't think about that now.

Because then, just then, as he watched this... this... vaporous devil, this... wraith without form, this ophidian mass, this pulpy cluster of – ah hell, this... *Thing* that was blacker than night and just as mysterious fluxing in the shadows, it was then that a magical sight struck his skull like a mason's hammer. He rubbed his eyes. He couldn't believe it. Just above and to the left of that, well, that *Thing* was a rectangular breach in the rock. Strange he hadn't seen it before. Horizontal and cut with right angles, it was the work of a capable mason, no doubt about it.

Now he could figure it. Them dumbasses had dug down in the right spot, but their dynamite charges went too deep. He had fallen right past his target.

"I told those dumbass sonsabitches."

But they never listen. He chuckled lightly but only to abate the rising violence inside his mind.

Well, this was it, by gods. He would ape out of this goddamn wedge and get to that opening if he had to break his own damn legs to do it.

"Time to uncork this bottle."

With a mighty swing he spiked his pick-hammer into the side of the tunnel above him and seized the handle with both hands. He bore down and pulled with every bit of strength, every bit of grit, every undying rage that burned within him, all of it detonating at once. His molars chipped, and a spray of spit followed a grisly roar. Slow and steady, dreadfully slow, his legs raked free. He drew himself up and balanced against the side of the vertical shaft. He bent his busted knee, and it felt like a round of buckshot was fired into him.

He shook it off and stood tall and reached over and gripped the lower ledge of that rectangular shaft. Fresh air was a good sign. Some ole vein of the ventilation network, he figured.

He eyed the shaft. Damn. It was barely big enough for a young'un, let alone a man his size and disposition. It was barely big enough to get his shoulders in and at least fifty feet deep. He'd have to slither through on his belly to the other side. It would be tight, damn tight, but he could do it. That's what he told himself anyway.

He took a breath and advanced into the shaft. Once inside, he tried not to think how much it reminded him of a coffin. Or a mouth – with teeth – chewing him to bits.

And it was then, just then, that another vision appeared to him. A vision of a newborn babe still wet from its mother's innards slipping like an oyster down the throat of an ancient giant. He picked up the pace. Sweating like a hog in July. Wriggling and squirming flat on his belly like a giant white worm. A damn funny sight for a man his size and disposition.

He tried to think of something else. Anything else. So he reckoned on how easy it was for that no-account brother-in-law of his, Dodgy Bill Dalton, to persuade him to quit that bucket-of-piss brothel and head out west.

"I gotta go," Bill told him.

His voice was soft and husky, flavored with a faint Kentucky accent that leaned toward the dramatic.

"Ever since your sister, my darling wife, sweet Annabelle, succumbed to that ole devil's grip," he clasped his hands as if in prayer, "that accursed fever, well, it's just been so hard on me. You know how hard it's been on me, Jake." He took a pull of whisky.

Truth is, Bill was a peculiar character: long and lean with the stare of a vagabond, half dead from opium addiction, but possessed of the immaculate neatness of a dandy and the extravagant taste and style of a carnival frontiersman. He was a hustler. Crafty as a rat in a house full of cats.

"I've tried to be strong, I have," Bill said, "but with my injured back and no work, I can't feed my boy. The bank's taking the house." He took a pull of whisky.

"Kansas City," another pull of whisky. "I've shat in donkey stalls with more decorum and grace."

Then whisked his moustache ... dramatically.

But he wasn't finished.

"If I could've been here when she died I would have," he said in his most convincing tone.

"You know that," he looked to Pinebox. "You know I would've been here, Jake."

He took a deep drag from his cigarillo and held it.

"I loved her." The smoke surged into his nostrils.

Pinebox couldn't find any lie in it. Bill had loved Annabelle in his own way. Not enough to keep him from the opium tents or gambling parlors or brothels, but he loved her just the same.

"It's just... blast it." Bill pursed his lips to the side and expelled the smoke.

"My luck's run out."

His eyes went dark.

"It feels like the walls are closing in," Bill said dramatically.

Back in his present situation, Pinebox continued squirming like a giant white worm and thought, "the walls closing in?"

"Yep, as soon as I get outta here I'm gonna punch that luckless sumbitch right in the nose."

Truth was, Bill was weak. On the day Annabelle died, he was laid up in the opium tents getting his load-on with the Celestials. On the day she was buried, he was squirreled away with Fat Sally, the meanest, most hideous whore in three counties, losing his last red cent at the Faro tables. And worst of all, he just abandoned his boy.

Otis, the boy who wasn't there. Pinebox found him hiding under the bed. He hadn't eaten; he hadn't moved. His eyes were sunk back in his skull, and his skin was so pale you could see the blue veins wiring through his scrawny limbs. But he couldn't think about that now. Not now.

That poor boy stayed curled up beneath the bed for a week, sleeping on a pile of his mama's dresses. He stayed there until Pinebox brung him a feral pup.

"This little fella ain't got nobody to care for him," Pinebox said gently. "And ole Cookie wants to make hound stew out of him, but I wouldn't let him."

Otis inched out belly first.

"Can I have him?" Otis asked with tears in his eyes.

Pinebox nodded and Otis ran to his uncle. He grabbed hold of that pup and held it tight while the critter licked the dirt off his cheek.

"Let's get you something to eat," Pinebox said through a big ole grin.

And with that, they walked in afternoon rain back to the brothel. Otis didn't undress or even finish his lunch. He and the pup fell dead asleep, sopping wet from the rain, curled up on the bed.

As soon as the wild women of the Orchid caught a glimpse of that little blond boy, they nursed him with more care and attention than he'd ever received. They combed his hair, washed his clothes, and bought him dime novels and hard candy at the General Store. Pinebox wasn't sure if his sister would approve of these painted surrogates, but it was the best he could do.

Down in the tunnel, Pinebox sighed deeply as he remembered his dear sister. Fair skinned and doe-eyed, with hay-colored hair and the heart-shaped face of a forest pixie. Pretty enough for most. But everyone assumed she was mute or dim because she never spoke and wrote on a little chalkboard that hung from round her neck.

Truth is, she stu-stu-stuttered. A proud woman, she never solicited a handout or a hand-up. Even so, when Pinebox came around for Sunday dinner, he'd leave a little money in the breadbox. Not much, but enough.

It was weeks later that Pinebox went back to check on the house and discovered some of Annabelle's things were missing – an ivory comb, a gold brooch, her Sunday dresses – things Bill was probably trading to the Celestials for skag. Pinebox removed what remained – her Bible, the chalkboard, a tintype of her and Otis – and brought everything back to the Orchid with him.

Broke and without any trade, ole Dodgy Bill was forced to clean up and make that walk-of-shame down to the Orchid, hoping to make amends with his kin. Bill approached cautiously. Some of the women hung from the balcony and waved flirtatiously at him. He pushed back a smile and straightened his jacket.

Pinebox was on the porch cutting an apple with a knife too big and dangerous for the job.

"Jake, may I approach?"

Pinebox pushed a wedge of apple between his lips but never once looked at Bill.

"The thing about a bad apple is," Pinebox said to no one in particular, "it's rotten to the core and the worm always gets out."

"Jake. On my honor, my lips haven't touched a pipe in two days." He placed his hand over his heart. "I'm sober as a judge."

Pinebox continued to skin that apple and imagined it was Bill's throat. He curled his lips and spit a chunk of chewed apple on the toe of one of Bill's fancy boots.

"I've heard that before."

Bill eyes fluttered. He smiled delicately and wiped his boot on the back of his frilly pantaloons.

"I still have a bit of liquor now and then," Bill confessed, "just to ease my ailing back, but – my hand to God – I'm done with those Celestial devils."

Pinebox cut another slice of apple. Bill straightened his coat. "Please, Jake. I'd like to see my boy."

There were tears in his eyes. Pinebox hesitated. He thought about it. He should just slit his throat and bury Bill beneath the outhouse. But he didn't. He couldn't. Blood is blood.

"Otis," he called out with a mouthful of apple. "Come see what the cat dragged in."

Otis emerged with a dreadful look in his eyes. He marched to his pap, picking up steam with every determined step, heaved back and kicked him in the shin. There was a crack like an axe biting the side of an oak. Bill lost his air and dropped to a knee. Pinebox smirked.

Bill grimaced and whispered, "I'm so very sorry, son." Dramatically.

Otis ran back inside. Bill stood up slowly.

"Jake, I need to speak with you." He dusted off his knee. "It's urgent."

Another slice of apple.

"I ain't feeling so talkative these days."

"Yes, I understand, but I think you'll want to hear what I have to say. Let me buy you a drink."

It was hot as the hinges of Hades out here. Pinebox could use a drink. He sheathed his knife.

"Otis, get my hat. Your pap's gonna buy us some drinks."

They took a quiet stroll down the muddy thoroughfare to the Last Chance Saloon. Two stale beers, a bottle of sour mash, and one sarsaparilla later, Bill convinced Pinebox that indeed them walls was closing in, and they should take that long trek to a rotten place called Gnaw Bone.

"Leave Kansas City to join up with a hive of bushwhackers and dumbasses to slave away in the Loving Brothers silver mines? That don't sound too agreeable."

But then Bill showed him a wanted poster for the murder of Bug Fenton. Pinebox was thunderstruck. He snapped the yellow paper from Bill's pink fingers and stared in awe.

"I'll be dipped in sheep shit," Pinebox said. "That possum-skinnin' dumbass had indeed hollered sumthin' about having a brother in politics right before I put my boot in his eyehole, but that mouthy sumbitch was warned not to hurt them girls again."

"Dumbass shoulda listened," Bill smirked. Pinebox grinned. "Best we skin outta here and slip the noose."

So it was that very next day Pinebox purchased a wagon and paid the fare for the caravan under the promise that Bill would ante up his share once they arrived. That was the plan anyway.

O' course, the whole trip Bill told his tall tales to anyone who'd listen how he'd been married thrice before, his first wife taken by renegade Chickasaws (so he said anyway), and the other succumbed to consumption (so he said anyway), and now, again, he was a widower. He made sure everyone knew he was a widower – especially those easy pieces of cake sent to restock the brothels.

Oh, poor Bill, yes, *pour* Bill another drink… that's more like it.

Yes, widower for the third time. At night he'd plop down on his blanket, cross his boots and hold a bottle tight to his chest as if someone might take it away. He'd stare up at the deep bend of night sky with his face half-cut in a fool's grin. Pinebox would always wander off to check the horses. He'd heard it all before, and he was sick with it. Undeterred, Bill would commence a recital of his long list of Homeric conquests: how he saved Napoleon's cousin once, how he gave the ree-ward to an orphanage, how he took down a grizzly with a slingshot, how he was blood-brothers with Chief Iron Bull, and on and on. O' course, he'd always end it with how he and Pinebox was gonna strike it rich with the Loving Brothers, and how Otis would be his heir, on and on. Then, Otis would rise from the blankets like a ghoul from the grave and whisper excitedly, "Tell me about Horse Head, Pap." And Bill would slur through them ghost stories Pinebox was trying so hard not to think about right now.

Back in the present, it had gotten tighter in that shaft. But he wouldn't be deterred. Only a few more feet anyhow. He pushed on and scraped through until he fell face-first into the open passage. He landed hard and heavy. He stayed still, catching his breath and steadying himself from the fall.

He lifted the sour air into his lungs. There was a graveyard fragrance, damp and moldy. His headlamp flickered, casting strange shadows on the earthy walls. Them words that weren't his were worming through his mind again.

"Young flesh. Fresh meat. Blood for lust, for power. Blood, yes, blood heals the wounds. Foul liquid. Suckle sweet."

He sat up, and his lamplight chanced upon a pile of collapsed rock. He inched over and sifted through. There was a bloody sock, a chisel, a pair of gloves, and a broken Davy lamp. He looked around the chamber. The timber supports lined the mine like a ribcage.

He moved on. One tunnel was completely caved in. Another led down a slope where it broke off and divided into other passages. It looked like a colossal hive.

"Otis," he hollered, "it's your Uncle Jake. I've come to fetch ya." No noise save for the trickles that dripped to the brown earth. He pressed on. One of the tunnels ended in a blank wall. He doubled back to where it split off and dropped down to a single knee. Frustrated, hungry and exhausted. It felt like he'd been down there for days, lost under the world. He wished he'd brought a canteen.

He plucked his helmet off and used it to gather water that dripped from the walls. He sucked back a mouthful; it tasted sour. He spit out the rest and wiped fever-sweat from his brow. He coughed and held the helmet-lamp out to see what he could see. Tunnels and cavities winding off into the dark. No signs of life.

(…the name)

He stood up and a burst of cannon fire went off in his knee again. Damnation. He pressed on, searching the blackness of the catacombs for Otis, the boy who wasn't there, through tunnels and broken shafts, turning sideways when it narrowed, bending over when he had to, wandering in and out of jagged channels and dead ends, doubling back and triple checking. But there was nothing. He was exhausted and feeling hopeless when a slow groan rose from the depths. The fine hairs at the back of his neck stood on end.

"Steady," he told himself, "mines make noise. The timbers creak. The walls shift."

He took a moment to get his bearings and spotted that goddamned awful *Thing* that had followed him into the underway. It was now a collapsing cloud of black filaments. The sight frightened him, but he wouldn't show it.

"You hang around like a bad smell," he sneered and coughed up something hideous. But that

Thing didn't even flinch. And then it sounded like that goddamned awful Thing had said something. It sounded like *"slawwwg"*. Whatever the hell that meant. But he couldn't think about that now.

He was about to throw a rock at it when his lamplight illuminated tiny footprints trailing off into a smaller shaft. He had to follow.

He told himself those little tracks were muddy, not bloody. He eyeballed the walls. There was – something – near the entrance, clotted streaks of – it looked like – well, finger-painting. He looked closer. There was words, matted words, smeared with gore. "Missed her hiss," that's what he could make out. He heard a little giggle.

"Otis?" The words fell heavy from his lips.

"Is that you, boy?"

There was silence before and silence after. Then, the vague sound of padding footsteps.

"Hey now," he tried to sound cheerful, "we gotta getcha back topside so you can care for that pup."

That feral pup was the only thing that had made Otis smile in the last year. It brought the color back to him. It was strange. Otis' skull smiled even when he didn't. Pinebox would never admit but, at times, Otis seemed to fade away, ghostlike. His flesh would be as clear as a bell jar and all the cabling and architecture of his insides would be visible. Funny how he never paid much attention to it before. But he couldn't think about that now.

"You don't want ole Cookie to make hound stew out of her, now do ya?" He waited. It had worked before. But there was nothing, nowhere. Nothing but that *Thing*. He looked back at it and said, "Looks like we're going in."

He felt a chill deep in his bones and his boots moved on without him, one after the other, following those bloody footsteps deeper into that smaller shaft. It was tight. It was nerve-wracking. It was a tiny lair beneath the world.

Inside it felt even darker. The passage narrowed and scraped his big barrel chest. He pushed on. The back of his shirt caught on something jagged. It felt like a bear claw. He jumped and shook free and moved deeper into the shaft. He noticed it was descending and wiped sweat from his neck. The snaking cavern widened, and his pace quickened. The rock changed color at this level. It was red as raw liver.

There was a scratching noise behind him. He turned. It was deathly black. Then, in the dim light of his headlamp, the vaporous *Thing* slinked across the wall. For a moment, it was about the size of a polecat, but then it spread wide and vanished into the dark. A snapping sound like bones breaking. And then it rematerialized. It was closer and hovered just outside his light. He tried to make sense of it. This *Thing* that followed him, that had evaporated only moments before, weren't no rat, nor bat, nor spider; it weren't no damn rattlesnake neither. This formless goddamn – *Thing* – this undulating membrane of liquid black filaments, whatever *It* was, haunted his every step.

(the name…)

He tried to catch it in the yellow disc of his light, but it was too swift for him. It didn't scurry away like some dang'd cockroach when you open the shitter door; it just, well – it slithered – no, that's not right – not exactly – it squirmed, no, it fluttered – like the last wisp from a dying campfire – yes, all right – better. It fluttered.

And every time he angled the headlamp toward the inky apparition, the damned evil thing recoiled from the light, fluttered to a different spot, and waited for him to make a move. It was damned aggravating.

He tried again, hoping that if the Thing didn't notice his stare, it wouldn't flutter. So, aiming the headlamp straight out at a fixed position, he averted his gaze covertly. And it worked. And it was horrifying.

His eyes trembled over the ghastly form of this lightless, eyeless golem. Not only did it have a matted braid of maggots where its tongue should

be, but that goddamned awful *Thing's* mouth was girdled by an upper row of square teeth that looked almost – human. There was a dragging sound in the dark. Then he thought he heard his name. A gelatinous voice, deep and croaky.
(the name, say it, say the name.)

An iron scream burst up behind his teeth. He wanted to run, he wanted to race harum-scarum out of there, but he couldn't. He was petrified.

The *Thing* disappeared and reappeared down the tunnel. His eyes narrowed, focusing. And that, well, that *Thing* slowly formed into the silhouette of a man. But not quite a man, more man-shaped. The darkness came alive, and shadowy fingers winnowed to long spidery claws that came together to form a steeple, that parted and waved him forward, motioning him deeper into the earth. Then, there came a hissing, no, a cackling, then the *Thing* pulsed, grew bigger, and eclipsed into the dark.

A heavy thud behind him. A low growl in front of him. The smell of rancid meat. He pulled a big knife from his belt. The blade glistened like a silver fang. It was sharp enough to cut buffalo hide, and the hilt was carved from the tusk of a wild boar. He stood up slowly, holding the knife in front of him with one hand over the other.

"What are you?" he barked at that Thing.

Cannon fire in his knee again. *He cursed all the dark devils of the godless black.*

Maybe it was his own blasted shadow. Maybe his mind was deceiving him. But maybe, his mind hissed, it was one of them lost miners slowly going berserk in that devilish dark.

"Hell, any man I come across now will be more fucked than a whore at closing time. That's for damn sure."

There was a curious tug inside his gut, and his body slumped like the bones had gone out of him. He leveled himself against a support beam and noticed his hand was trembling. He wished he had some tobacco.

"Otis. Come on, boy. We got to go now."

His mind wobbled and quivered. How had he let Bill, of all people, talk him into coming to this infernal place? A warrant for the murder of Bug Fenton was suitable incentive, sure, but he could've gone anywhere. Why was he drawn here? To this desolate pit? To this forsaken land? Why did he come to... to... (the name of the camp slipped over his lips like a forsaken soul) to GNAW BONE?

(gnawbonegnawbonegnawtheboneGNAWtheBONE)

From the depths arose a harrowing cry. The damned demon, the smoldering, well... *Thing...* suddenly appeared and dashed down into the pitch. For a moment, he could see the faintest trail of its passage before the weak luminescence dissolved into nothing. He tried to speak but could only think of Otis, the boy who wasn't there. Several breathless moments passed. Then, an agonizing shriek shot through the cavern and all fell quiet. Deathly quiet. But he couldn't think about that now. Because then, just then, his headlamp dimmed to almost nothing. He rapped against the side of his helmet trying to bring the fire back.

"Come on," he whispered and hit his helmet again.

"Not now. Not yet."

It flared and faded then settled to a weak glow. He sat flat against the wall and wiped the back of his hand across his lips. It was getting hard to breathe. He tried not to think about the blood colored drag-marks that led deeper down the tunnel. He tried not to think about starving to death. About being buried alive.

He wanted to scream. He wanted to beat and break the craggy rock until his knuckles shattered or the mountain gave way. He wanted to turn tail and ape up that jagged throat until his fingers bled, until his lungs heaved in a blast of fresh, sun-soaked air. But he couldn't. He had to find that boy. The boy who wasn't there. He shook his head again, violently, as if something was trying to crawl inside it.

He suddenly remembered Samson, that old drunken piano player at the Orchid, priestin' at him.

"Jake," he'd slur and play a chord, "there are none so blind as those who will not see." Pinebox wished he could choke that soothsayin' sumbitch right now.

Somewhere in the distance a muted sound rumbled to him. The walls shook. Rubble fell and timbers split. Pinebox closed his eyes and feared them dumbasses up top were using dynamite to blow open another rescue tunnel.

"Only true-to-the-core dumbasses would do such a dumbass thing as that," he said to himself. Then again, them boys had all the sense God gave a duck's ass. He wouldn't bet against it. Or maybe, he thought, they was sealing off this tunnel, burying him alive.

He wiped dust from his eyes and hoped like hell them dumbasses would forget they lit a stick and blow they-selves to smithereens. He slowed his breath and tried to think of something else, anything else. How he wished he had a map of this winding underway, so he could make his way back to the surface with the boy he was searching for, the boy who wasn't there, who wasn't anywhere.

Another quake boomed through the cold cavity of the earth.

"Damn them all to the fires of Hell."

A large block of granite dropped down in front of him and split the walls like dinner plates. He covered up and almost prayed. Soon, the rolling thunder of the avalanche faded back to that familiar graveyard hush. Then, a hissing – no, a cackling – a goddamn glottal of murmurs rose up in the dark. Whatever it was, or said, seemed to surround him, modulating everywhere at once. His soul shivered. Deep and dreadful. Then, them words that weren't his returned to him.

"Kiiilll," it s-s-said. *"Crush the skull. Break the neck. Grind the bones. Eat the gut."*

He slowed his breath and had the oddest sensation that something had come real close and, well, it felt like – it sniffed him – the same way he would sniff Sunday dinner. He jumped up.

"Come on, goddamn you!" he said through his teeth – knife at the ready – but nothing came.

He stared into the dark. Shaking. The rage rose up, and he stabbed the knife hard into the dark earth. It felt good to destroy. He did it again and again. Wet mud trailing with every stab, splattering his square jaw and the powerful muscles in his arms. In the dim light of his headlamp, it looked like blood. It looked like a slaughter. He stabbed until the panic dimmed, until another word emerged. A dull sound with a grim melody.

Suicide. That was the word.

Suicide. Suicide. Suicide. Suicide.

It came again and again. Clawing like a ghoul from the grave into his throat and to the tip of his tongue. He dropped the knife and slapped a hand over his mouth, fearing the word would leap out and force the knife to act on its own.

(Open the gut, slice the throat, skewer the heart)

But he smothered it. Sucked it back into his gullet and held it there until it dissolved into nothing. He slumped to the floor and did the only thing he could do. He hoped. He hoped the lamp would last, he hoped to hear from Otis, to hear from anyone, above or below. But mostly, he hoped that foul, deplorable *Thing* had returned to his blasted nightmares where it belonged.

He closed his eyes and let his thoughts drift again to the surface, to those puddle-sucking dumbasses and their dastardly deeds, to that unutterable evil squirming just below the brume of his raging soul, to a life that seemed to exist a thousand years ago.

He chuckled softly as he remembered some onwards verse, "Here blooms the legend..."

Exhausted and lost in thought, he didn't notice the goddamned awful *Thing* gather over him like an oil slick and pulse for locomotion. He didn't notice its smoky filaments worming around his busted leg, cocooning him. He didn't notice his lamp slowly surrendering to the eyeless black. Or the translucent form of Otis, the boy who wasn't there, surveying the grisly scene in ghostly silence.

"I shoulda ended them royal dumbasses when I had my shot," Pinebox spoke in a faraway manner. He felt drunk. "And rode like hell outta this shit-hole."

But no, he had to step up. His double-crossing, underhanded, skunk-sucking, dumbass brother-in-law was pressuring him the whole meeting.

"Jake," he called him proper, "you gotta do something."

Three days ago a main vein had collapsed, trapping eleven men and three young boys. Otis was one of them.

The Loving Brothers refused to let anyone go in after them. It was too close to winter, they said, not enough men or resources, they said. Horseshit. It was just cheaper to dig another hole and start over. *(should'a slit their throats)*

From the back of the meeting hall Bill leaned in, his hands trembling, dope sick.

"Please, Jake," he said dramatically, "it's your sister's boy."

Pinebox slouched back against the wall, lit a cigarette and pondered. Bill had to have an angle. Maybe a ree-ward or some hush money? Or maybe it was simpler. Maybe losing Annabelle back in KC wounded him more than he let on, and Bill couldn't stand losing his only son. Maybe.

But Bill was the feculent dumbass who brought that young'un here, who sent him to work in that mine so he could nurse his "injured back" with the Celestials. No, something didn't reckon right. But Pinebox couldn't figure it.

He looked off to the horizon. The long rays of the setting sun crowned the mountains with golden fire. He soaked it in as if this was the last time he'd ever see such a marvelous sight. A breeze drifted in, it lifted leaves from the trees, smelled of campfires and coffee, and carried a soft thrum from mysterious places.

He exhaled a long line of smoke and looked back to Bill. He wanted to beat that pipe-sucking sonofabitch to a broken sack of meat and ride like hell outta this forsaken shit-hole and never look back. Ever.

But what if Annabelle was staring down from her starry perch and saw Jake abandon her only boy down in that awful dark? Somewhere in his mind was the sound of a bullet being chambered. He took a long drag and let it swirl around his insides.

"Ah hell, blood is blood."

(blood, yesss...blood)

He exhaled the smoke like hellfire, pushed to the front of the meeting hall and stood before the Loving twins. What a sight they were. Same dandy duds, same dull expression. Identical in every way except Jebediah was a ginger redhead with a dark beard, and Jesse was a brunette with a ginger beard. Big men of industry? Hell, they weren't as big around as one of his legs. They looked like a couple of mutated children seated behind that heavy oak desk (much too ornate for this part of the country) in matching Arthurian thrones with red velvet headrests and dark-wood arms that stretched out into carved lion paws.

Maybe it was the way they twisted their mustaches in tight little curlicues, or the cowhide boots laced up to their knees. Maybe it was the thick sideburns sprouting down their cheeks, but to Pinebox they looked like a couple of sprites right out of a storybook. He couldn't figure it, but there was something awfully familiar.

He pushed back a bray of laughter and cleared his throat. The twins stood up to face him. Their eyes widened the faintest bit as the dark shape of this tremendous man loomed over them like a thunderstorm. They were a good foot and half shorter, even on their tippy toes, even in those fancy cowhide boots.

Jebediah muttered something to Jesse, who quickly covered a large book with a pile of charts. The old tome was weathered and had strange markings inlaid in the cover.

(signed in..in..)

"I think we've heard enough," Jesse said nervously.

(…inblood)

"There's nothing more we can do." He looked to his Mephistophelian doppelganger. "Do you concur, brother?"

Jebediah nodded. "I do." His voice cracked.

"Then this meeting is adjourned." He banged a tin cup on the desk and waited. Jebediah slid a guarded hand into his vest pocket and scanned the crowded room. There weren't no mistaking the nature of these men.

Pinebox was unmoved. He used his considerable size to telegraph a message to these two ridiculous looking dumbasses that whatever control they assumed they had belonged to him now. He smiled, and both men instinctively receded.

"Gents," his voice rumbled quietly, "my name's Jake. Pinebox Jake." The light seemed to dim.

"Like these men here, I work for ya. And before things get outta hand, and y'all set something in motion that can't be reversed, I just want y'all to think for a minute. Just …think."

The twins froze.

"Y'all forget where you at?"

(the name)

"This here's Gnaw Bone. Ain't no sheriff nearby, no Marshall, no Pinkertons neither. It's just…" he stopped and smiled. "You two soft-scented dumbasses and me and my men."

The foremen bit their lips. Dumbasses. Everyone knew that utterance, oh yes, bellowed over the grime and raw thrum of the camp, bellowed like a Cyclops pillaging a village. They knew what was coming.

"Men willing to risk anything," Pinebox continued, "and I mean anything, to get back what they," he corrected himself, "what *you*….lost."

(crush the skull…)

He planted a massive hand on the only thing separating him from these two shivering dumbasses, that mighty oak desk covered in charts, and felt a fire rising inside his mind.

(break the neck…)

The twins swallowed hard. Nobody ever had the salt to stand up to them before, especially unarmed. But Pinebox knew their kind.

"I know your kind," he said, "weak-bodied, loud- mouthed, arrogant shits, phony brave with an armor of inheritance. I've flattened dumbasses like you two dumbasses my whole life. Hell, back in Kansas City they paid me to do it. I'd beat dumbasses like you two dumbasses with their own belts – some with their own piss pots."

Something strange came over Jesse. It wasn't just a fear of the impossibly large man towering over him. There was something else, something nefarious, something awfully familiar.

"Sometimes little men like to act big. They like to hurt them working girls. Just for, I dunno, the godless fucking delight of it I guess. Well, that's where I come in. See, I'm a rough man used to rough ways. I don't tolerate nobody hurtin' them girls. That's a lesson them dumbasses learnt mighty quick. And it didn't take much for them to start screaming and carrying on, shrieking and gibbering like they were on fire. Crying for their mamas and whatnot."

He leaned in as if to share a secret.

"But I'll tell you a secret. I like it. It's fun. Dumbasses, who think they own the world sobbing on my boots, begging me to stop breaking this or stomping that. Sometimes they'd faint before I could really get going so I'd carve a little x on their cheeks like I was branding livestock. Just for… I dunno, I guess just for the godless fucking delight of it." Pinebox winked and his face creased into a cruel smile.

(eatthegut…)

His palm rested on the big knife that hung from his belt. Jesse felt his knees give. On his cheek, beneath his hairy sideburns, was a slight scar in the shape of an x.

(youngflesh…freshmeat)

The large eyes of the twins grew larger. A tiny rendering of Pinebox stained the watery plane of their baby blues, conjuring terror like a wild beast trussed with a frayed rope. Jebediah wanted to speak, but his tongue was paralyzed inside his skull.

"Let's talk plainly about those young'uns," said Pinebox. "Even if by some miracle they survived the collapse, even if the air stays good, even if they remain calm in that awful dark, the stories the ole fellers spoke about ancient devils and cannibal ghosts are haunting them young'uns as they wait for us to come get them."

(draintheblood)

Jebediah elbowed Jesse as he wilted with a fear that mirrored his own. But Pinebox wasn't finished.

"Two winters ago, you lost your first crew down in that mine and you left them there. You left them in that dreadful dark. Those men, who you sent into the earth that winter, who broke their backs to fill your pockets, those men went so hair-tearing mad in that hopeless dark, they ..." the words stopped at his lips.

"Those men," he cleared his throat and he felt his stomach flutter, "when the rescue crew finally reached 'em, they found those men gnawin' on their own kin, fathers on sons," he looked Jesse dead in the eye, "...brother on brother."

A vast shadow burst up behind Pinebox.

"Did you think we was just gonna let you make that same mistake twice?"

Jebediah gripped the derringer in his vest pocket and trembled. Two shots weren't enough.

"I know the evil that haunts the minds of men," said Pinebox. The shadow blasted out in great curling tentacles. The twins felt dizzy. They gripped each other's hands. Everything seemed to disappear as if a spell had been cast. Everything...but Pinebox.

"I know some men are made of fire," he bellowed. "I know some men are made to be burned."

Then – as if in a nightmare – the shadowy tentacles thrust out at the twins, coiled around their matching cowhide boots, and ripped them down into the earth. The shape of Pinebox receded above them. They half expected to see a roaring fountain of hellfire ripping upward as the grisly sounds of suffering and the spectral faces of cannibal ghosts soared up around them. Faces of men they lost, faces of hate and fear, faces that made them fearful they'd slipped into that bedlamite break between this world and the next, a locus of nightmares and madness. But they couldn't think about that now.

They spun round and round in the deep entrails of the earth, whirling like sewage down a drain, but as quick as it came, it ended. They found themselves ripped back in the present, curled on the floor, breathless and defeated.

"Does that proffer suitable incentive?" Pinebox sneered. The shadow pulled back.

The foremen shared a confused look. They weren't sure what to do so they crossed their arms and kept quiet.

"Y'all look like bettin' men," Pinebox said to the twins. "Be honest now, would you make that bet?

That you got the backbone to stop us from retrieving what's ours?"

The twins were paralytic. It felt like they'd been whirled in a tornado and slammed against a wall of rock. Pinebox lifted both men to a standing position by their fancy collars, one in each hand, and shoved them against their thrones.

"Would you?" But they didn't answer.

He patted their chests and plucked a cigarette from Jebediah's fancy shirt pocket and lit up.

"Praise the Lord and place your bets. I'll take your money with no regrets," he said through a big shit-eating grin. He sucked back a deep drag and raised his eyebrows, acknowledging the tasty exotic tobacco.

"Now, let's assess the sitcheeation," his voice rose, and he exhaled into their empty faces.

"Knowin' how much losin' them boys means to us. Knowin' how you chose to dig up on Horse Head when we all opposed. Knowin' how some of us might blame you two dumbasses for this, well…" he took another drag and ground the fancy smoke underheel, "if we's being honest, you know, honest Injun, then all this is just *ceremonial*. We don't need permission."

He shoved the heavy desk to the far side of the room. Books and charts soared through the air like birds. Glass lamps shattered, and arteries of oil and fire bloomed across the floor. The twins screeched like rats in a trap and hid behind their magnificent thrones. Pinebox swelled his chest and swung his arms wide like a gunfighter.

(blood is blood...blood for blood)

He pivoted and shouted to the whole room.

"Now some dumbass is going down into that mine. Who's it gonna be?"

THE GIRL WHO WASN'T THERE

The first thing you need to know is that she's *unusual*. The next thing you need to know is just how unusual.

Scorching embers swarm the tiny form of eight-year-old Paisley Grim. An impish feather of flame gathers from the cascading cinder and hovers before her. *The night darkens. The world stands still.*

"I want it," she says barely above a whisper.

"All of it."

There's a sound like bones breaking, like steam escaping, and the small flame detonates in a long, liquid spray of copper fire.

Rooftops light up, dry fields smolder, and beads of fire twinkle like Christmas lights on the lean limbs of the evergreens. Waiting. Everything smells like a campfire.

Unaware of the danger, the simple people in the vast valley below have no idea what's coming. They assume they're safe, they're comfortable in their humdrum, and do what they always do. They drift through the hours distracting themselves with nightly regimens of cigarettes and cheap beer, TV and rotgut, dinner burning in the oven, numb eyes staring at dust.

A cold wind whips through her hair. "It's time," she says softly to the western sky. And then, just then, the simple people in their simple homes hear a peculiar scratching (like fingernails against a coffin lid) in the walls, beneath the floorboards and in the corners of attics. Their dull faces pucker as if they've smelled something foul. Then a mass exodus erupts: rats and cockroaches charge from garrets and cupboards, spiders and silverfish scuttle through cracked walls swarming toward windows and doors.

The wind gusts and swirls around the valley. Dry leaves lift from dead branches. Tiny cyclones of trash and detritus twist up and dissolve to dust. The trees bend at their middles, listening intently to a tiny voice on the wind.

"And you, my beauties," her voice is as gentle as a kiss, "no more chains, no more cages. You're free."

And then, just then, pets turn on their astounded masters, clawing and biting – chewing through frayed ropes that bind them to trees. Livestock break out of pens and stalls, slip their trusses, kicking and bucking – trampling fences and escaping kill chutes – before racing away to the migrating multitudes.

Paisley spies a rusted weather vane atop an old barn. It spins as the wind gales in from the east.

She grins.

"Your turn," she says to the eastern sky. And then, just then, all the birds of the forest amalgamate into a colossal flock that spirals away like a black cyclone.

The vane spins again.

"And now you," she says to the northern sky. And then, just then, enemies as old as the earth, predator and prey, walk side by side through the dark forest.

"Yes, all of you," the words come to her slowly, and all the squirming, slippery life of the Black River slithers downstream as the rushing river begins to boil. The weather vane spins faster and faster, until it seems like it might helicopter away, faster and faster as the wind powers down through the valley. But then, as if in anticipation, it slows to a gentle halt.

"Now," she beams to the southern sky, "it's our turn." Her voice is hungry and tense.

And then, just then, flames rise from the dark earth like an infantry waiting for war. Behind her, a long seam of fire splits into two praetorian columns capped with little ivy wisps. Around her, a ribbon of flame circles and rises like a ring of golden cobras ready to strike.

At one time, she believed she could make the world more beautiful. More magical. But that time is over. She wants to cremate her misery and all those who fathered it.

She nods and the school explodes, sending filing cabinets and wooden desks spinning end over end into the sky. Reams of paper and burning books swirl in the updraft. Next it's the abandoned hospital, then the church, the pesticide factory, the jailhouse, and the trailer park. But it isn't enough. The churning infernos splash out to fixed positions and detonate like miniature atom bombs.

They can't ignore me anymore.

Paisley Grim, the girl who wasn't there, who wasn't ever anywhere, the strange girl with the strange name, the girl no one noticed. Her name implies pattern, decoration, something exotic, clutter even, but if one were to ever look at her – really look – not glance or skim, but stare, you know, really drink her in – well, aside from big moss-colored eyes and long curls of blood-colored hair – you wouldn't see much at all. This isn't a slight, I assure you. It's a fact. There isn't much to see. She's a quiet girl, acutely shy, but that's not it. Her corporeal light is fading from existence. Pigment evaporating. But no one notices. Even when her skin is translucent as an ice sculpture, when she is nothing more than a ghostly form inflating her clothing, no one notices. Even when the opposite happens, when she becomes something so mystifying she defies belief, when her skin is smooth and reflective as a drop of water, when she glows like a Christmas tree, like a swarm of fireflies, like a doll illuminated from the inside, even then, no one notices. Not her family, not her schoolmates, no one. Paisley Grim, the girl who wasn't there, who wasn't ever anywhere, no one noticed...until now.

"I want their bones scattered in the valley like an open grave," she says in a terrible voice, and the fiery hordes bow before blasting out in great flaming arcs and scattered explosions. Heated winds jet past her in the concussion.

She mumbles something, a spell perhaps, an enchantment maybe, and ghostly fingers steam up from the cold country.

"Burn it all."

The flames linger – briefly, minutely, deadly silent – before marauding down into the burning valley. Buildings and homes combust, trailers and sheds implode as if being crushed by an invisible giant; propane tanks burst and ricochet into the sky.

She whispers another word, an old word, one that will never be uttered again, and everything vanishes in a blinding flash of golden light. The burst ignites her dark eyes and blood-colored hair.

"They thought nobody could stop them," hisses the voice leaning in from the dark.

"Well," she says, barely aware she has spoken, "I'm *nobody*."

Down in the town, vehicles explode, and people race from their burning homes into the streets. Some spray themselves with hoses and leap into boiling swimming pools trying to escape the inferno, but the flames are alive and jump from person to person with hideous delight.

"If you play with fire," she whispers playfully, and the forest ignites in an orange plume.

She sits as a child would sit, carefree and cross-legged, on an old stump atop Horse Head Hill. The air is thick and difficult to breathe. But she gives no thought to it. Instead, she stares in silent wonder at the raging carnage below.

"Not so mean now, are they?" she thinks to herself. "Little matchsticks, heads aflame, running helplessly, dripping liquid fire from their bones."

Then comes the bloody hammering of fists and kicks against doors that have been sealed shut, against windows that refuse to break. Doors and windows that will never open again.

She imagines a white-hot flame glowing in the deep recesses of her soul devouring every splinter of mercy. Then, long filaments of fire tinged with gold blast out and corkscrew through the valley. She stays still for a moment and exhales.

For as long as she can remember, she's been ignored. Well, mostly ignored. There were times when the bullies at her school zeroed in on her. They seemed obsessed. Possessed more like it. Drawn to her. Like spiders to a fly. Sharks stalking blood in the water. They wanted to hurt her, to punish her, to humiliate her and prove they were superior. They wanted to extinguish her uniqueness. They thought it was funny to be cruel. They wanted her to react, to cry, to beg, to kiss their muddy boots. And even though she never gave them what they wanted, they kept pushing and pushing.

(It's their fault)

They yanked her hair, shoved her into puddles, tripped her in the cafeteria and elbowed her in the stomach so the teachers wouldn't see. They made fun of her clothes, of her glasses; they made fun because she was poor, because she was different, because they could. The adults were too busy lamenting the loss of their youthful dreams to ever care about poor Paisley Grim. Perhaps she reminded them how common and simple they were, of their horribly ordinary lives, which they pretended to ignore. Small places like this tolerate the slow destruction of anything unusual. And she is…unusual.

Well, they wanted a reaction, even demanded one, and she's ready to give it to them.

"I've been silent for too long," her voice is rising. "You talk so much but you never listen." Her voice rumbles like an earthquake.

"I've silenced your tongues behind your teeth," her voice echoes into the valley like a thunderclap, "and now you will listen to a choir of carnage sung by the suffering of those you love." She speaks in a commanding tone much too ancient for a child so young.

"You will listen to their screams stabbing again and again into your empty hearts. You will beg for mercy. You will beg me to stop. But I won't listen. I'll do as you did. I'll speak in fire with a tongue of vengeance. And you'll listen to the slow murder of the world. You'll listen to your eternal hopelessness. You'll listen. Because it's my turn to talk." Her fists tighten like little mouths.

So many times she had begged for help, prayed for mercy, but no one answered. *No …One.* But some…*Thing* did. *"This is what we want,"* a voice hisses presently, a voice hanging in the dark. It was Darkness that had listened, and it was Darkness that had answered.

"This is what we've always wanted."

In the distance a great blackness looms,

slowly erasing the soft facets of the flickering stars. It's moving closer, gathering speed, coming into focus. An impenetrable wall of boiling smog. The massive flock of coagulated birds is instantly incinerated as it tries to spiral over it.

This presence, this ancient power gathering over the burning land, this whatever it is, this *Thing* has locked minds with her. She blinks, hooding the fear with heavy lids and white lashes, and gazes up at the malicious black vapor. It's here. Hostile and nameless, ripped from the sunken depths of her shadow mind. The *Thing* that lives in empty spaces, that hides in dark places and gnaws on the old bones of the world.

She loses her breath. It's as if an invisible noose has looped around her neck, dragging her earthward. Words that aren't hers rise up.

"Before light, there is darkness," the voice rumbles with dread, *"waiting for it."*

She feels as if the world is turning upside down, and her soul is trying to crawl out of her pores.

"No light can stop it," it says, *"no light can escape it. All things must return... to darkness."*

Tracks of smoke drift down in ever-darkening shapes that scrape the earth with ghostly claws. In the distance, streams of magma are beginning to boil over the dark land. As the wall of oily smog moves closer, a detonation of craters leads the way like the footprints of an invisible god. The earth rumbles. Fire detonates everywhere. Her ears ring with a piercing scream. High and thin, the sound is soaring from the burning village in shrieking bursts that rocket up and powder down like ghastly fireworks.

They don't care about you. It's their fault.

She starts to speak but hesitates. "This isn't right," she tells herself. "This is supposed to be my turn. You said so." But this monstrous, abominable... *Thing* is undeterred and gloats over the captive town. She's breathing faster, like a wounded animal, and battles against a primitive ache to annihilate them all in a quick flash of molten violence.

This doesn't make sense. What is this, she can't describe it, this horrible *Thing*, this monstrous *Nothing*, marching over the valley? This isn't her beloved Mr. Hiss who kept her company at night, in her dreams, in the back of her mind, always present, ever there, forever.

Her army of flames is now colliding with the smog. The flames whip up into the boiling wall, and the black clouds mash down trying to extinguish them. She struggles and shakes with rage. "Stay still," she whispers. Wisps of smoke vent from her mouth. And the fire ceases to advance. The colossal wall shudders and stops too.

The burning wreckage is suspended in her eyes: the dark clouds of ash rolling like an ocean, the red rim of the moon rising over the edge of the charred horizon, the smoldering muddle of black poles and red charcoal of the forest, the sky streaked in blasts of crimson, gold, and black.

A long pillar of smoke rises from her position. "You promised," she says to the wall of smog, "you said I could do this myself." She speaks as a child speaks on the verge of throwing a tantrum. "It's my turn. I can do it." She looks away. Sullen.

Beside her, shielded by the mighty roots of the ancient stump, a small flower remains unburned. A wildflower. She smiles. Her mom used to call her that. "You're my little wildflower, Paisley." Yep, that's what she'd say all right.

She reaches for it. The vibrant petals are wilted and curled. A single tear, silver as moonlight, slips down her cheek and falls on the stem of the flower. It immediately blossoms and stands tall in the smoking chaos. Her heart flutters and her body radiates glittering halos of indescribable color. She wipes her cheek with her sleeve. The rage pulls back. A subtle gravity carbonates the moment. Her feet pull up; the ground drops away; and she levitates with the floating smoke over the scorched palm of the earth.

"Remember what they did and why they did it," says a voice belonging to no one. *"To control you. To erase you. To destroy you. They've taken so much; we can take some back. Fight fire with fire."*

She shakes her head as if engaged in some interior debate and refocuses on the flower. She tries not to think about the fetid stench of burning hair or the screams of agony rising all around her. This is really what she wanted. To bring beauty to this ugly world. But this is their fault. The wall of burning smog resumes, cremating everything in its path. The vast migrating herd she liberated is now trapped and running over each other trying to escape it. Her head perks up.

"Not them."

"Nothing can escape."

"Not…them," she says stoutly.

With a motion of her hand, the smog ripples and divides down the center like a cell replicating. Another motion and the smog parts like a drape – like Moses commanding the Red Sea – and the herd races through alive and free.

She smiles but only briefly. The wall coagulates and shoots up into the atmosphere and curls over the burning land. Long strands of smog reach down and caress her. It has resumed control.

The wildflower wilts again. A shadow descends over her heart. Her thoughts are occupied by another mind, a scorching cloud of rage, a shifting loop of liquid black filaments.

"Remember how they dismissed you, ignored you, bullied you. You must defend yourself. Hurt them like they hurt you."

She shivers.

"Hurt them like they hurt you. Hurt them like they hurt you. Hurt them like they hurt you. Hurt them like they hurt you."

She places her hands over her ears, but it won't stop. Her mind is bombarded by wild memories, snarling recollections with jagged teeth dripping with blood and venom, distorted bodies armored with scales, fangs and claws ripping through her shaking soul. Memories of cruelty, of isolation, of hopelessness, and revenge. Of being pelted with mud, of being shoved and laughed at. No one cared, no one stopped them, no one helped her. No one but Mr. Hiss. She screams and the fire flares. She screams and the earth quakes. "Fine. Finish it." The words escape her mouth before she can stop them. Then, there comes a terrible, triumphant roar and the smoggy *Thing* mushrooms into the burning shape of a primordial god. She closes her eyes and the axis of this great and terrible form, this dreadful...*Thing,* clefts into a colossal mouth of roaring fire. People are screaming; they're praying; they're weeping and holding their children.

"Lava-bombs," she says barely above a whisper. The great Shape hovers for a moment, as if pondering her request. "Lava *bombs?*" She nods the command. Lava bombs. (She's eight) The great Shape hesitates a moment, twists and cannibalizes itself like a fiery Ouroboros and then meteors down great volcanic spasms of unspeakable power.

Paisley Grim, the girl who wasn't there, who wasn't ever anywhere, sits safely under a protective shell of shimmering light.

"They'll say it was a lightning storm," she speaks in a thousand otherworldly voices, a chorus of lost souls. "They'll say a natural gas line exploded or the pesticide factory blew the whole place to smithereens. They'll say *Nobody* was to blame. And they'll be right."

The scorching bombardment continues until there's nothing left of the village, of the people or their cruelty, ash-shaped people covering their eyes, holding their children, scattered like debris, nothing left but a smoldering pit in a formless world, and Paisley Grim, the girl who wasn't there, who wasn't ever anywhere.

"Because… I… am… Nobody."

She opens her eyes – blank as stones – and a

pressure wave detonates from her position. It circles the valley nine times before diminishing to a soft breath of warm air that flutters gently through her hair. The dark shape dwindles to a tapered wisp.

(They should've known better)

Silence washes over the smoldering slag and spirals of soot drift back to their hovering master.

The night darkens. The world stands still.

Bewitched by the shivering madness of an untamable power, bewitched by the fires of unfathomable vengeance, she doesn't notice the *Thing* vanish liquidly into her shadow or her body dissolving to a charred pile of ash.

It's their fault.

MADE MAN

It ends where it began. Inside this empty chamber, staring at empty parchment, waiting for the way to come to me. I've returned to this ancient place hoping it would inspire, hoping it would motivate or incite an ignition, a flight, a release of my mind's bow string, anything to purge the words from my aching soul. And hopefully, with any luck put an end to all that I've begun. But I never mastered the skills of the scribe or possessed the fervor of the bard. I'm a man of the sword and simple pleasures, not the quill. But I must try. Perhaps wine will help. Wine always helps.

Alas, another miscarriage of progress. Empty bottles at my feet, on the table next to me, tipped like fallen trees, and still nothing stirs but my ever-lengthening shadow. The quill arches over the page. I want to write my story, I try, I ache to do it, but my hand hovers motionless, mocking my foolish heart. Damnation! My soul screams for the muses to illuminate me, for a gentle kiss on the head, a whisper, a blessing, a direction, but they have forsaken me. So here I sit, inking my lonely thoughts in the gathering dark. The remaining candles have burned down to little mouths of quivering wax and darkness gathers round me like a heavy cloak.

A beam of moonlight has formed a silver circle on the adjacent wall, illuminating the empty spot where chains once hung, where she once wailed in the surging swarm of madness. My eyes drift to the arrowslit and perceive a slow movement of shadow near the marble crypt. I pretend it's an animal but I know it's her, wandering in endless night. My beloved Elsbeth, as she was, still exists in the moonstruck wilds of my imagination. But here, where she decorated the air with laughter, and brought fire to a cold place, in this very room where we spent many nights cradled in the arms of love, I am forced to face what she has become. Shrapnel. A savage, jagged phantom of the woman I loved. The golden veil in tatters, the opalescent gown ripped and bloodied, dark eyes wet with hunger, the heavy steps, slow and steady, the hiss of animal mutterings, the graveyard fragrance of old rot, a shriek in the lonesome night.

I want to tell you of being awake but not alive, of seeing the world change without being able to change with it, of watching everything you love fade and diminish to dust. I wish I had the scholarly means to explain just how torturous this is for me. I want to tell you, not because I'm arrogant, though they say so, but because I need to free myself from what I've done and I need you to know the reasons why. I must admit, just writing these few passages has relieved so many burdens from my heavy soul. Perhaps you will scoff. So be it. An apology from a devil must seem so inconsequential. I don't blame you. I doubt you'll even accept it, let alone believe it, not for the crimes I've committed, not for who I am, or what I've become. Honestly, I don't know when or if this will be found, there's so few of your kind left, but if you're reading this I want you to know I am truly sorry. I never imagined my actions would have such devastating effects.

So it is, after over a thousand years of existence, I've chosen to seal myself in the lower chamber of this forgotten place that I pray will remain so. I have imprisoned myself, brick by brick, a slow struggle of will that only martyrs know, here in this secret rest to protect you from me – to pay for my sins, of course, but also to end my misery.

But before you judge what I am doing as a coward's surrender, understand I have spent a century slaughtering and butchering my way through this plague, searching the world for a cure. But, alas, I have failed.

So, here I am, writing in the thieving dark, confessing to the empty night. Slowly, yes, but still confessing. And if I am to empty myself of my secrets I should tell you I'm writing this in the ancient Adamic tongue – the first language of the human race. I am using my own blood for ink and the pages are made from human skin. You will understand why as we proceed. But I hesitate further for fear once the barrier is breached, the story might expel from me the way bats detonate from a cave and this will end up nothing more than the fevered chattering of a forgotten bedlamite. I know, I know. This is just a clever game to delay what must be done. Meander about with the words, pretend to have lost my faculties, construct this confession in an ancient language, and avoid the task by slowly collapsing into suffocating dread. My mind betrays me. Truth is, I'm ashamed. But I mustn't delay much longer for there isn't much time.

From the other side of the high oak door I can sense them drawing near. The familiar howls and moans, the slow, heavy steps, the creaking of old bones, the thick stench of rotten flesh.

The door is fortified, of course, locked and barricaded, but it will not hold as their numbers increase. And they will ...increase.

So I must just get on with it, to the best of my recollection and ability, stop behaving like some jabbering blatherskite and write! Write, damn you, write!

I apologize for this intellectual stutter. I've spent so many years alone that I'm used to disagreeing with myself. And, yes, it could be the wine. Oh yes, the wine. I worry it's had the contrary effect of my hopeful intention. But I do not wish to ramble any longer. I feel the inspiration rising. So we begin. My final confession and emancipation, in the common tongue of my people, Adamic, of course. It will be up to you to translate it but a small price to pay for what I'm sacrificing. Enough now. Yes, begin.

My first memory is of light, a soft, heavenly luminescence that splintered at its limits and radiated a cascade of misty halos too brilliant to describe. A mystical nimbus that lifted me out of the cold infinite empty and injected me into being. I was aware only that I existed. Time was inconceivable.

And so it was that impressions shifted into thoughts and thoughts drifted and coagulated into consciousness and I felt my presence slipping into a body, aerating the limbs and adjusting the muscles, as if being dressed.

My senses opened like a flower. The first sound was the steady, heavy thump of my heart, followed by the wet slosh of blood flooding flaccid veins. The next was the slow, cyclical rhythm of breath opening my body to the world. My mind uncoiled like a serpent, and I became aware of this body, of arms that branched into hands that were balled into fists, of strong legs bifurcating, thick with muscle, of a neck that held my head, of eyes that were blind, and of a mouth that could not speak. My eyes fought to focus as one might do immediately upon waking from a dream, but light was all I could perceive. The next sensation…was pain.

Tiny electrical charges, like a million microscopic lightning strikes, surged through my fingertips. The pain came again, fiery thorns racing up my arms, but then dissipated into nothing.

And then, as I floated vaguely within the infinity of my own mind, exploring the slow revelations of existence and the variant hues of phosphorescent light that flooded my eyes, I was hit by a sensation so excruciating I hesitate to summon the memory. But for you, dear reader, I will.

Without warning, several flashes of molten energy pierced through me, igniting every nerve, charging in and exploding out. My lungs were crushed of air yet somehow I screamed. A fierce howl erupted from me and formed a modulation that I would later understand to be an ancient word used by sorcerers meaning "stop" or "desist." It did not work. Another strike bore through me. I was paralyzed and suffocating.

Again and again, harpoons of energy penetrated the entirety of my being. With each strike came a burning pyre of information that illuminated my mind in the endless dark. Again and again, pain and information filled out the hollow spaces. It was too much for my embryonic mind to take and I sank into the warm blackness of oblivion.

After a time, how long I do not know, I woke to that familiar heavenly glow but this time there was a strange noise rising all around me. A gelatinous warble modulated and penetrated my senses in waves that I soon understood to be a form of communication. As it continued, I somehow comprehended that this exotic instrument, this repetition of concussive grunts and broken melodies, was a voice presenting language. I tried lifting my head but could not. I instinctively searched for the source but my eyes remained gorged with light.

The words ricocheted through me as if I should know them. I tried desperately to make sense of them, to hold on to them as they passed through, but nothing stayed. As the words went, emptiness followed. I became dizzy and nauseous. I began slipping away from this place, the light dimming, as if being swallowed.

The voice, thankfully, continued, calm and commanding, an anchor in the chaos, and as the words drifted through the deep caverns of my mind, they pollinated me with understanding and in an instant I comprehended.

"All is well," the voice was saying, "take your time. We have plenty of it." It pulsed as if underwater.

"Can you hear me?"

It was clearer now; the voice rose from the left and my head followed. I still couldn't see past the haze of light.

"Yes, over here. Very good."

For several moments I struggled to make sense of what was happening, to force my eyes and ears to sculpt the messages it received into something I could understand.

Again the information bolted through me. The golden glow that had blinded me clustered to consolidate shapes into form, then shifted slowly to pick out detail. The voice, yes, the voice; it was the key to unlocking everything. The images soaked into me as rain does into soil. Behold. I understood. Above me, a circle of fire, a massive chandelier, yes, lit by an assortment of candles, rows and rows of them. And around me, high walls of chiseled rock. To the right were arched entryways leading into shadow, and to the left small windows held tiny orbs of night.

A massive mirror was maneuvered above

me and reflected the entire room. I could see. I wasn't just a gathering sentience trapped inside a meat prison. No, I understood now, this vessel, this body, my body, belonged to me! And these bright blue portals from which I saw were my eyes that were in my skull attached to my neck that was bound and restrained, along with my limbs, to a massive slab in the center of a massive room.

But who was I? And why was I here? In this place? Held down this way? Suddenly, I was seized a new sensation. Shivers of fear and anxiety gripped my being. My wrists pulled weakly at the restraints and I tried again to speak but could not. I didn't know how. Again, just outside the ring of light, the voice persisted.

"What you are experiencing is normal," it said. "Try not to resist."

The words hissed from the umbra, circling slowly, careful to stay in the dim.

"Acknowledge if you understand."

The voice seemed to hover above and below, everywhere at once.

I tried to understand what was happening; believe me, I did. My imagination was born in those uncharted moments, and I succumbed to the grim terrors of my awakening. Talons of anxiety ripped into me and I heaved and pulled against the heavy restraints, but I was too weak.

My eyes peered into the half circle of shadow around me. Nothing moved. Then, as if the darkness gathered and pushed into the light, a form developed. It was, what I soon understood, a man. Tall and lean, he was not prone like I was; he was upright. His skin was not exposed like mine; this man was draped in long purple robes that drifted like smoke. Beneath his heavy hood, I could make out the harsh lines and shape of a face. A short beard edged his jaw and his dark eyes burned with a fierce hunger.

"Can you speak?" His voice was raspy and powerful. I did not answer. I did not know.

"Grip my hand if you understand."

I felt the bony clutch of his fingers slip over mine. I lifted my head and looked down the length of my body. I was nude, my milk-colored skin hairless and new, and the left side of my body was covered in symbols. They weren't merely painted on, as I first thought, but were tattooed into my flesh.

I could feel the power in my muscles as they flexed beneath my skin. My understanding of this room, my body, this man, our divergence and likeness, everything, spiraled from infancy to clarity in what seemed to be a matter of moments.

"Grip my hand," he said again.

My hand jumped with electrical reflex and

closed around his. He smiled and his eyes lowered to mine. He released me and walked around the slab, keeping his eyes fixed on me.

He spoke to himself of my movements, my body shape and size, murmuring details of the hour and minutes, things I couldn't clearly understand but that seemed important. And somewhere in the darkness, I could hear the sound of scratching – rhythmic, matching his every word. It was the sound, I later understood, of a quill on parchment. Someone else was with us. Someone unseen. My mind raced with possibilities. How many others could there be?

These queries stayed with me only momentarily. His mutterings, these mysteries, seemed meaningless compared to what I was beginning to understand. It was if I was waking from amnesia remembering a world I had long forgotten. My blood was carbonated with joy! A thrill ran through me and so possessed my mind that all reality was lost, or was it gained? I did not know! I did not care! My mind was once empty and now it was gorging on a feast of sensory data! I recognized the scent of perspiration and the charge of ozone in the air, the salty tang of saliva running over my tongue, the grit of enamel from grinding my teeth, the weight of the restraints fashioned from iron, yes, iron! A metal! That held me to the granite slab, a rock! And then, a cool breeze blew over me, a breeze that had traveled from exotic realms, which carried the faintest trace of animals, incense and campfires. I could see ghostly tendrils of smoke rising from the many candles scattered about the room. This room. In a castle built long ago by master masons. We were in the mountains. Someplace ancient. I understood gravity, exothermic oxidation, a lightning strike that lit up the night sky. I knew, somehow as swift and powerful as thunder, I knew what they were as soon as I perceived them – all but the man. He remained a mystery. He placed a hand over my chest in a reassuring gesture.

"You are programmed to do this. Try to speak."

My mind knew what he wanted. I was to mimic the noise coming from his mouth. The language he spoke was a relic from an ancient race.

I will not presume to bore you with the time and process needed for me to learn to speak. I can tell you that the first sounds to emerge from me could have been mistaken for the cries of a dying animal. My tongue flapped about like a fish plucked from a stream. And the noise, the howls and moans that belched from my lungs proved most embarrassing.

The Robed Man, as I knew him then, used

all sorts of incentives and motivation to spur proper speech from me. It was during this time that I learned my flesh would not cut or burn. Nor do my bones break as easily as yours. It takes time and effort. The blade, the flame, the hammer: I am durable, he said.

You will have to understand that I was still learning who and what I was, what I am, and what I was meant to become. I remained exceedingly timid during that early era. I recall being frightened of a mere spider as it crawled over me while I was restrained on the slab. I was completely unaware of my power.

At night, as The Robed Man walked the long corridors of this place, reciting spells, theories and formulas quietly to himself, I would spend my time alone, secretly practicing the words I heard.

Once I learned and became fluent, I chose not to reveal my ability, not only because he had ordered me to, though I must admit rebellion played into it a bit. It is my nature, you see; it's part of my coding. But also because I feared what he might do if I possessed this magic of language he so desperately wanted me to have. It was difficult to hold back. I wanted to speak with him. I wanted to know who I was, what we were, why I was here, and why he seemed uninterested in freeing me from those damned restraints.

He claimed he would release me, let me run in the fields and play in the forests that surrounded us if I would utter but a word. I didn't believe him. My instincts warned against it. Besides, I reckoned I would learn more about him, this place, and my purpose, if he felt he could speak freely without worrying I would understand.

Now, forgive me a moment, but I must interrupt. It is strange to be back here in the very room where I came into existence. Strange to be using this slab, where much of my early days were spent chained down, as an instrument of emancipation, a writing desk. The same slab that doubled as an altar for my wedding – the same restraints that bound me and would one day bind my beloved during her transformation. The same terrors multiplied by my own hand, by my own arrogance, fueled by fear and blinded by love. I find myself staring at the cobwebs in the darkened corners, pondering the stale smell of dust and rot. How this vacant it feels. There's no time for sentimental rambling. More wine. Yes, and then back to it.

My silence continued to frustrate The Robed Man. One rage displaced another and on and on it went. The sun rose and the night came many times. I endured and suffered, but I refused to speak.

It was just after the winter equinox that

everything changed. It had been days since he had attended to me. I lifted my head to the limit the iron restraint allowed and looked for him. He was seated at his worktable writing and murmuring something about "oxygen deprivation, frontal lobe thrombosis, necessity of partial lobotomy, cremation," words and phrases I had never heard before, but the way he spoke them alarmed me.

And then I perceived the soft rhythm of padded steps approaching from the far corridor. I looked and there, hobbling through the entryway, something like us – but very different – appeared.

I could smell it before I could see it, wrapped in rags that stunk of disease and filth. The Robed Man did not look up from his parchment as he spoke.

"What is it, Slog?" he said, agitated. This filthy thing, this Slog, dropped to a knee and bowed his head. He addressed The Robed Man as Maker, and then with permission granted by a single gesture of the Maker's hand, spoke with mechanical grit beneath his eloquent voice.

"Most Powerful, Most Gracious, Most Revered, dear Lord and Maker, I offer congratulations on Specimen Cronus. A masterful work, sire."

He was motioning at me.

"You didn't come all the way from the

basement to tell me that, did you? What of the others?"

Slog bowed his head even more deeply.

"My lord, it is with deep regret and boundless remorse that I must report to you that Specimen Icarus failed to recover from the procedure and has perished during the night."

"Burn him."

Slog swallowed hard and cleared something sticky from his throat.

"As you wish, but, forgive, Maker, it is," he slurped back a jaw full of spit, "my penitent duty to further report that Specimen Elohim has gone quite mad." He paused before letting the next words out. "He's killed and eaten Specimen Ur."

I peered hard into the darkness to see this Slog but could distinguish little except a misshapen skull, short legs, round chest, and corded arms capped with long, spidery hands. All of which were as pale as a drowned corpse.

The Robed Man grimaced.

"You were supposed to keep them muzzled." The heavy wheeze from Slog's labored breath punctuated the tension.

"Endless apologies, my lord. Indeed, I did as you asked, but Elohim is quite clever and was able to remove it. Ur fought valiantly, he did, but Elohim is much too strong," he stuttered, "much too strong, too strong, and was able to overpower him."

"Burn them all. Empty every cell."

Slog shook his head knowingly. "As you wish."

I watched Slog raise his body higher on one side as he turned and limped to the door. A beam of sunlight illuminated him long enough for me to see the long scars and healed wounds that spread over his face like a quilt. A mysterious ticking and grinding of gears clicked sequentially deep within him.

He looked back at me with great concern. His eyes were black marbles dotted with a single ivory point. He paused for a moment, as if to say something, and then vanished into the far corridor.

The Robed Man glanced up for a moment, saw that I was watching the empty space where Slog had been and said, "You should rest."

And with that he rose and walked to his private chamber. I remained unmoved as the day surrendered to night and the candles burned slowly to ash and darkness enveloped the room, pondering this Slog. What is Specimen Cronus? Is that what I am? Or who I am? And what of these others? Elohim and Ur? I tried to decipher it. But failed. I drifted into a deep sleep. Dreamless at first, but then my mind's eye flashed a silhouette, a gigantic form standing over a crooked corpse pooled in black blood.

It was then that I woke and a shriek detonated from deep within the innards of the castle. And then a voice, closer, whispered, "I apologize for the screaming."

It was Slog, seated in the dark, his dark eyes burning. "Don't worry. It won't last. The furnace is quite efficient here."

He sucked back a mouthful of drool. "It's the smell that will linger. The smell always lingers. You'll get used to it." He blinked and became one with the dark.

"I try to make it easy for them," his voice floated in shadow, "I cover them in garlands of beautiful flowers and wash their limbs in perfumed oils. I even gag them with rags soaked in opium. Blindfold them. I bind their feet to their hands. I even add extra fuel so it goes quickly. But they still scream like this." He shook his head. "I often think the screams are their way of insulting me. To make sure I know I'm not doing a good job. I don't know. Our Maker says this is impossible because these creatures – creatures like you – are incapable of higher thought. Still, their eyes," he inhaled deeply, "I don't like them looking at me when the flames jump on them."

I felt as if I might go mad. I wanted to be free of this place, to see beyond this room, to escape the dust and rot and stink of burned skin. He rose up next to me and stared. And then, beneath his congested breath, that soft ticking and clicking of gears and cogs came again. Sunlight glinted off the windows and I could see now how he was knitted together. The crosshatching of scars, the mismatched clumps of hair and odd patches of flesh stitched together like a scarecrow. Some were freckled while others were pale as moonlight. Some were different races altogether with red or blue ritual tattoos decorating the skin. Other tracts were clearly pocked with disease. Some were youthful while others wrinkled and shriveled with age. A large scar bisected his face from left to right. His lipless mouth was covered in large staples that formed a false smile from cheekbone to cheekbone.

"I am called Slog," he said with pride. "I named myself. One day maybe you will have a name, and if you're very lucky, our Maker will allow you to choose it." I think I must have recoiled because Slog lowered his voice and tenderly placed his long hand over mine.

"All this suffering is a gift. He is correcting you. Can't you understand? You're not like the others. I can see it. You just need time. No, you're not like the others. Are you? Yes. You understand."

He leaned to my ear, "I think you can speak."

He checked the doorway to make sure we were alone and continued, "I've heard you. Whispering in the night. I know you can speak and I mean, just look at you. The Maker is getting better at the formula. You and I, we're not like the others. Those rotten things down in the cellars." His face puckered as if he'd tasted something sour. "Those mindless drones and beastie golems. I detest them. Our dungeons are overrun with these hideous, pathetic things... well, I mean," he paused, "they were hideous."

And, as if on cue, a scream detonated from the furnace. Slog snorted back and swallowed.

"The first batch, the middle batch, the last batch, they end up as kindling. And unless you speak, you will too. And he'll continue to create these hideous things. Nature has long stood by her mistakes but not our illustrious Maker. No, he will not abide them."

Slog raised a long finger to punctuate his point. "He's raising the evolutionary altitude of the species. You must accept your purpose. You must try very hard. Please, you must speak. Don't be afraid. Yes. You must. You must. Otherwise," he pointed a long, white finger at my head, "he will cut open your brain to locate the defect, and he will make a drawing of it. He's made lots of drawings. Lots of drawings. Of course, I'll write it down, and then he will burn you." He stopped and moved closer. "Well, to be precise, I will burn you."

His lipless mouth joined the iron staples in a smile exposing square teeth of polished copper. He stifled a laugh and then his smile collapsed as if to fend off some insult.

"But I will find no great joy in it, mind you. I am not a sadist. Not a sadist. It's my job." He turned and limped around the table. "I have torched piles and piles of these half-men. Their ashes rain down on the outer village like snow in winter." He was on the other side of the table now. "I have been with the Maker for a long time. Trust me, you don't want to spend what life you have bound to this hunk of rock, do you? Of course not; and I know what will set you free! You must speak! Speak. Not mimic like some bird! Say something worth hearing."

He raised his hands on either side as if to pick me up but balled them back into fists. Then his long left hand slapped the table like a wet fish.

"It's such a gift he has given you. Such a gift." His voice dropped and he sputtered excitedly, "Not like me, like this, sewn together like a sack and filled with rotten things. No," his eyes traced the shape of my body, "you, you are a masterpiece. A-a-a-a masterpiece."

He grunted and then took my hand and crushed down with a powerful grip.

"We are brothers. Bbbbrothers."

He stared at me for a moment and then his temperament changed. Eternal sorrow dripped from this chimerical creature.

"I don't mean to be so dramatic. It's just that, well, it's been so lonely over the centuries. So lonely," his black eyes returned to mine. "Oh, I need you to be the One. I know I shouldn't grumble, but I grow tired of burning those unripe creatures, of watching life erupt and recede. I grow tired of watching him cobble specimens from the dark, pouring your bodies into patterns like melted wax, imprinting you with instinct and wisdom and infecting you with the immensity of his soul! Do you understand? His soul! It's so beautiful when he does it. So intimate. Gentle as a kiss. He leans over ever so gently, just above your lips, and exhales a wisp of his powerful spirit into your lungs. The black vapor almost seems alive, and I suppose it is, it is, yes, it is, as it enters your lungs. He did the same for me but alas, I have no memory of it. But these half-men do not show any gratitude at all. They stay mute and savage. They do not appreciate his gift. They abuse it. And then they are given to the flame."

A large flap of skin peeled forward, exposing a gray stretch of skull. He turned and collected himself, and smoothed the piece back into place like someone correcting a wig.

"But mostly, you must speak because after he's succeeded with you, he can finally fix me." He quickly corrected himself. "Not that I'm broken. I'm not broken. What I mean is, he can finally finish me."

We shared a moment and then he whipped a dagger from his belt and held it above me. For a moment I thought he'd gone insane and meant to drive it into my neck or open my gut. He smiled devilishly; he knew the flash of the blade startled me. In his other hand, held between his long fingers like a spider wrapping a fly, he presented a shiny, red apple. He plopped down on the table next to me and began cutting small wedges and pushing them between the staples covering his mouth.

"I would offer you some but you'd probably choke."

He smiled and enjoyed the juicy sweetness of the apple and sucked the pulpy mash down his gullet.

"I don't think you even get hungry yet, do you? Oh, just wait until you discover food. Oh, the joys of sweet cakes and roasted meat and wine! Oh my! The wine! You must try it!"

He disappeared for a moment and returned with a golden vessel in the shape of a bird.

"Stop breathing and open your mouth."

I reluctantly did as he commanded and felt the rich, warmth of the wine fill my mouth and spill down my cheeks. Slog chuckled.

"Now swallow. Push it down your throat."

For a moment I held the liquid in my cheeks, enjoying the richness of the wine soaking into my taste buds and drowning my tongue in flavor. I thought to myself, "Swallow? There's more to it? This is wonderful!"

"Like this, watch me…watch me."

He took a large gulp of wine and I mimicked his action. The sensation of the wine entering my throat and spiraling into my stomach was divine. I was so grateful for this moment. He did this a few more times, and I started to feel like I was floating, but I wasn't. He then hopped off the table, retrieved a book of fables from the bookcase and hopped back beside me. He sat very still and began to read aloud.

When morning arrived, Slog was still reading, and we had finished off a few vessels of wine. The Maker burst into the chamber, his long robe flowing behind him like fire.

"What are you doing?"

"Reading to him," Slog answered penitently. The Maker charged over and ripped the book from his long fingers. Slog dropped to the floor, his eyes cast at the feet of the Maker.

"Endless apologies. Please, please, I did not mean to offend. I was only trying to help."

The Maker's voice dropped to a hiss.

"Silence your tongue before I cut it out! Return to your duties at once. My chamber pot needs emptying."

"At once, my lord."

Slog stood slowly. We shared a smile and as he limped past, the Maker was overcome by a spell of madness. He kicked Slog in the back, sending him reeling and tumbling to the stone floor. Slog immediately balled up like a bug. The Maker grabbed a long cane and began whipping Slog. I pulled at the restraints in protest. The Maker's eyes looked to mine – something flashed in his mind – and the violence increased. He beat and kicked and whipped Slog until he screamed for mercy. But there would be none. I feared he would beat poor Slog to death. I grunted and moaned, pulling terribly at these immovable restraints. I cried out. A word, it must have been a word. I believe I sounded like a fool, as if my tongue had been removed, but the word I was desperately trying to say again was "Stop." I marveled for a moment and repeated it. "Stop." Then I perceived a laugh coming from him. My mouth stretched over my face, involuntarily, and I roared with rage, "STOP!"

He kicked Slog again, and then raced to me. His eyes burned into mine.

"Say it again. Come now. Once more."

I could not. I would not. Not because he ordered me to. He loomed over me, giggles turning into hysterical laughter, until anger swept over his face, and his smile shifted to a snarl. He spun away from me, marching quickly back to Slog, who rolled into the far corner.

"Slog will have to pay for your silent rebellion."

He dragged Slog by the silver mane that sprouted from the back of his head to a metal structure outlined in copper wiring and iron restraints.

Slog pleaded, "No, sire, please. I'll be good. Please, mercy, my lord, not the lightning machine. Not the lightning. Have mercy on poor ole Slog, please, not this."

He placed Slog's long arms in the restraints, turned some dials, dowsed him in salt water, and pulled a lever. The machine ignited and sent the dreaded lightning into Slog. He jolted like a fish on a wire as his body began to smoke, and the room filled with the reek of burned hair.

Over the screams and over the crackle and over the electric sizzle and soft thunder, the Maker cried out to me, "Speak again! Tell me to stop! Curse me to damnation! Confess your hatred of me! Declare murderous intentions! Just speak! A word! One word! Come now! I know you understand! Speak!"

It was if his words were fists. I felt a fire detonate within me. Before I realized it, I broke the iron restraints, sat up and roared at this man with a savagery that, later, would leave me staggered and troubled.

He stared at me with some surprise.

"Well? Come on then, fool! Speak!"

He pulled the lever again. The machine shook with greater intensity as fountains of electricity sprayed out in all directions. Poor Slog began foaming at the mouth.

I suddenly remembered I was free from the restraints and lurched up. My arms and legs flailed wildly. This was the first time I'd used them. The mechanics of standing had yet to fully process and I fell like dead weight from the table to the stone floor. I was shaking with rage. I gathered my balance and rose up. My feet wobbled and steadied my weight. And so I stood, as this man stood, back straight, chest bowed, jaw raised. I was at least twice his size. He was puny. Large head balanced over bony shoulders and skinny arms. I steadied myself and made sure he felt my presence eclipsing his. I took a single step, a shuffle really, and he stopped laughing.

"Speak," he said softly. So I said the only word I knew I could say. "Stop." The word thundered from me.

He dropped the lever, the machine fell silent, and Slog was still.

"Walk," he ordered.

His eyes were incandescent. I clamped my jaw and took a heavy step forward. My shadow devoured him. I stand just over eight feet tall. Agile as a jaguar, strong as a god.

I reached out with the intention of grabbing him by the collar of his robe, but it disappeared within my fingers like fine mist. He smiled, and I lifted him by his shoulders in a single, effortless gesture, from the ground.

"Do you understand what you are?" he asked.

I dropped him to his feet and said a new word, the only word that would form itself on my tongue, a simple word. His word.

"Man," I said.

My voice was deep and soft but sounded like I was choking on sand. I wondered for a moment if I had actually said something he could understand because he just stood there staring. I composed myself and tried again.

"I am," the words droned out of me deliberate and grated, "Man."

He looked upon me with what I knew to be pride, gripped my shoulders and howled to the heavens, "I've won!"

Forgive the interruption, but a few of my children have arrived early and since I'm just getting started, I don't want to be interrupted just yet, so I've reinforced the door. It should hold, for now. But now might be the perfect time for introductions. Maybe you already know. Perhaps you've solved the riddle. I've had many names, ancient ones. Some so old only the cold earth could utter them. But my given name, the one chosen by my Maker, the one tattooed down my left side in his private hieroglyphs, is Cronus Five, fifth of my name. The name may be unfamiliar – historical amnesia is common – but you know me. I am the reason your doors are boarded shut, your children locked away in the attic. I am the reason you pray softly against the biting dark. The reason you sleep with weapons at your side. I am the Maker of all terror and torment. And you know my children. They eat yours.

I know they accuse me of evil, of destroying

my Maker's legacy, and perhaps they are right, but I never meant it to be so. I did what I did out of love. I did what I did to end my loneliness. I had walked the earth for a thousand years and perhaps it was an overreaction, perhaps I was shortsighted, but there was never any malice in my actions. But I digress.

Now, before we proceed, you must agree to give me something that is equal value to what I am giving you. You must forget, for a time, the legends and fables that inhabit you. And allow me the opportunity to pull back the veil, to nourish your mind with truth and induct you into the impossible.

Like you, I was created from oblivion. This is why emptiness is always with us and we seek endlessly to fill it. Unlike you, however, I was brought forth into this world a fully formed man. My Maker created me. Not the way that you were made, not in that simple, sloppy, and buffoonish manner. I know the stories and fairytales about being made of mud, or of the man-beast in the labyrinth, or the tall tales of a monster amalgamated from the limbs and organs of dead men. But these are hideous lies. I was crafted like a sculpture. Just as Michelangelo begat David, I was molded and polished. Every cell, every hue, every infinitesimal detail was mastered by my Maker.

When he created me, he was well over 4000 years old. He had acquired wealth and land over the ages, which gave him the ability to move often and never be with the same people or in the same cultures long enough for anyone to notice he never aged or fell ill. His system was very organized. Decades here, an eon there, never surface, remain in shadow.

There was a time when he was human like you and knew the cold paralysis of death. But he was resurrected. Like mine, religions have adapted his story, changed his name, fixed the timeline so that it matches their creationist stories. My Maker, my misery. Legends, fables, myths, and fairytales. But I know the truth. He told me his origin story once, and only once, and warned me never to repeat it. I suppose it doesn't matter much now.

He told me he was born in a small village near a settlement you may know as Çatal Hüyük. Primitive by post-Neolithic standards but for his day, it was a bustling metropolis. One summer night, fire burst in the center square and as the people raced from their dwellings, a shape of a man stood in the blast zone, black smoke rising all around him. The men pushed their young ones back inside. Whispers flew like birds on the wind. The people spoke a name, "Magus Mundi," an ancient warlock, the last of the fire mages. He was so powerful he could kill with a single word. The elders bowed before him. They knew the stories; they knew his power. They told the soldiers to stand down, and Magus demanded gold, wine, and women.

My Maker, also knowing the rumors of what happened to the women, the bodies that were left, shriveled and dried like insect husks, grabbed his young wife's wrist and ran into the night. She screamed at a fire strike ahead. It was Magus materializing from the atoms of the flame. My Maker pulled his wife in the opposite direction. They ran faster and faster, the moon shining brightly over the desert terrain giving them ease to navigate.

Again, Magus appeared, flashing in a prism of color that fanned out as his body multiplied into a living wall of duplicates. There was no escape.

From beneath the black hood that covered Mundi's features, my Maker could see a smile curving like a silver dagger. Not a coward, my Maker released his wife and bolted directly at the demon. He ran until his heart pumped acid and his lungs brimmed with fire. Faster and harder, shoving his bare feet into the cracked earth.

Magus opened his arms as if to welcome an embrace just as my Maker sprung forward in a front kick, both feet aimed at the robed chest of Magus Mundi, and screamed bloody vengeance in flight. And just as his power strike was about to find purchase, a cackle slithered from the silver mouth of Magus Mundi. He clapped his hands and killed my Maker with an energy burst. The impact sent his lifeless body soaring high in the night sky, and then tumbling down a dune. His body was sucked dry and mummified.

Magus flashed back to the village carrying my Maker's wife. He seized the temple and ordered the citizens to provide for his pleasures. The men lined up like shepherds bringing lambs to slaughter, single file, offering their wives and daughters to him. The elders bowed their heads and carried gold and canters of wine.

Magus spent several hours inside the temple desecrating the altar and the women. The elders wept softly at the sounds of violence breaking the red stones of the temple. The high priest ordered musicians to gather and play at the steps of the great ziggurat to drown out the cries of the screaming women. They played through their tears, serenading the slaughter with epic compositions that did little to mask the despair.

Once Magus had finished the last of the wine and last of the women, he drifted into a deep sleep. The women that were left huddled together in the corner. Beaten and used, sobbing quietly as their sisters and daughters lay dead, scattered about, their bodies dried and mummified.

"Be silent," he roared.

They jumped as the words croaked from his throat and squeezed their bodies together like a fist.

Magus, annoyed, rolled from the large flat surface of the altar and stood over them. They tried not to stare, but the women had never seen anyone like him. Tall and muscular, the entirety of his naked body tattooed with jagged hieroglyphs. Forehead to wrist, face to ankle, row after row of cryptic symbols was written over him as if on parchment. Feathers and jewels were woven into his long black hair. He lifted a canter of wine to his lips and drank. Waves of crimson spilled down his braided beard and over his mighty chest. He pulled a fur from one of the mummified women. Her dried body rolled out in a puff of dust. He shook the debris away and wrapped it around his waist. He grabbed another canter of wine, stepped over the crying women, and walked out into the night.

Those outside the temple cleared a path for him. He looked upon these timorous people with disgust. Such despicable cowards to surrender so easily. He stopped, muttered a single word and the entire village fell dead. The air vacuumed from their lungs and they shriveled as if being dried from the inside. Magus, amused by his power, laughed and stumbled into the desert.

He searched until he found my Maker's body and sat down next to it. His drunken eyes stared down as he spoke to the lifeless corpse of my Maker. He leaned over and exhaled a wisp of black smoke into my Maker's ear. He sat back and stared into the distance.

"Your women are noisy." His voice was deep and raspy, salted with a strange accent. He took another sloppy drink. "And your men are cowards." A pause. "But not you."

His black hair draped over his powerful shoulders. He shifted his weight and swatted an insect.

Magus Mundi, the great warlock, was rough and unpolished. He was not a nobleman. His gestures were too awkward, too clumsy. He was a man of the wilderness.

He shifted closer to the body of my Maker and spoke to it with the intimacy of an old friend.

"Do you see that bright star moving over the sky?" He pointed to a comet glowing above the horizon. "Some say it's a god come to destroy the world. But he can't do that. He hasn't asked my permission."

Magus laughed heartily. He shook the last drops of wine from the leather canter into his gaping mouth then tossed it to the sand. He stared up at the streaking comet, his dark eyes swimming in a crimson sea.

"I'm going after him, this god, to teach him a lesson." Magus drunkenly looked at the corpse that was once my Maker. A scowl curled over his brow. "You're not listening." He placed his enormous hand over my Maker's heart. He began whispering as if in prayer, a pattern of words over and over, a spell, a curse, a conjuration of necromancy.

The wind gusted up in a powerful vortex. The landscape disappeared, washed away into a churning field of purple fire. My Maker's body shook and convulsed, his limbs popping open as if inflated.

His lungs opened and he coughed and gagged until a line of black smog, a twisting, looping swarm of liquid black filaments vomited from his throat and disappeared into a crack in the earth.

In that half-light of existence, my Maker said he was touched by the boundless coil of infinity. Magus, in his drunkenness, must have left out a word in the spell, or forgot to raise a protective barrier, because in that incredible moment, my

Maker was connected to the mind of the great wizard. In an instant, everything Magus knew was transferred with detailed comprehension into the dead but living mind of my Maker.

Suddenly, he could speak languages belonging to civilizations that he'd never seen. He understood mathematics, science, biology, alchemy, and magic, great things that someone like him was never supposed to know. As his lungs grew fat with air, my Maker resurrected from death as an immortal. He looked up at Magus who, realizing the mistake in letting his guard down, stood up and stepped back. He swayed to catch his balance and smiled down at my Maker who was fumbling back to his senses.

Magus continued his rant.

"Now, do you see that god up there?" Magus pointed to the sky. My Maker nodded, confused.

"He scares your people, you of the lesser races. And if they are scared of him, they won't obey me. So I must go to this god and destroy him in the sky." My Maker stared in a daze.

"When I return from killing this god, I will take back what I have given you."

And with that, a circle of purple flame erupted around the warlock and he was gone. Behind the chalk smear of the comet's tail appeared a line of purple flame, Magus, in chase.

After a time, my Maker regained his strength and returned to the ruins of his village. He no longer felt a connection to the people of his blood, to the lesser race.

As he stepped over the scattered bodies, some rolling in the wind like dried leaves, he cast an eye to the dual comets still visible overhead. My Maker gathered all the gold the cowardly elders had assembled for Magus and then proceeded to confiscate all the treasures from the temple. He went from dwelling to dwelling removing anything of value and packed it all for transport. Later, he piled the shriveled cadavers of his people in the center of the village and set them ablaze. There would be nothing left to remind him of what he once was and nothing left to connect him to this lesser race. He spent the night staring at the comet and the smaller purple meteor chasing it into outer space. His mind was now free of fear. These were not gods or demons floating overhead, only powers. He was left speechless by the beauty of the universe.

I think it's important to reveal that I'm using my blood as ink on pages of human skin for a specific purpose. They can smell it. And I can hear my children pounding against the great door with their broken fists and scratching at the hinges with their thick, hoofed nails. My blood has called my children to me and now they call to each other. The slow moan belching from their rotten stomachs has formed a single chorus that echoes like an array of nefarious foghorns. The louder they sing, the more will come, following the ghoulish call. This is my hope. The acoustics of the entry cavern will act as an amplifier, projecting their ghastly beacon into the atmosphere. The song will be passed until they will pack into the stone intestine of this mountain until they are crushed, floor to ceiling, paralyzed against the jagged rock and against the broken bodies of their sisters and brothers. And they will keep coming, a slow, unstoppable stampede that will force the great door to splinter and fall. Once it does, I will detonate a special mixture of explosives I learned from a master alchemist and incinerate everything, the villages, the slow, staggering armies of my children following the siren song, every Thing within a half mile. I do this for you. You're welcome.

But if you are reading this, then there is still hope. I've made an agreement of honor with a small group of hermitic monks that inhabit the surrounding peaks. One has agreed to protect this journal and disseminate it for me. Agreed, yes, for a price. For him, the reward was great. A talisman, holy in some circles, from the 8th century, encrusted with precious gems that somehow found its way to me. For me, a mere trinket easily given away for the reward it reaps. The plan is to seal these papers and the talisman in a tube of bamboo and drop them from the arrowslit on the east wall of this chamber. By the length and width, I can tell you that the arrowslit was originally designed for longbowmen. Once the monk has it, I will seal the arrowslit and wait for my immediate end. But back to my tale.

Many of the details of my Maker's long life remain a mystery. He has spent his eternity trying to master the gift that Magus gave him. To master it and best it. To reproduce this black vaporous soul magic. I can attest, as living proof, that he was successful. But let us not linger. Let's return to my story. To the morning Slog was beaten for his kindness. I think it's more interesting anyway.

Slog was in recovery for a month. The Maker used another, like Slog, to assist him. This other one was crippled and distorted, as if it had shrunk in a fire. As best I could tell it was also male. It did not speak but had the most beautiful whistle and would chirp songs of its own design in remarkable melodies that could rival the most exotic songbird. His main duty was to keep the cages in the dungeon clean. He was quite remarkable. He required no assistance from fire. At night he glowed from within like a firefly. The Maker called him Ignatius.

One day I decided to visit Slog in the infirmary and hoping to share another drink. I rounded the corner and was about to enter the chamber when I heard the husky voice of The Maker speaking in hushed tones. Though enormous, in comparison to you, I am light on my feet, as they say. It helps when hunting or in battle or when sneaking up on a conversation uninvited. I peeked inside the room. The Maker raised his hand slowly and, using his first two fingers, gently stroked Slog's bandaged jaw.

"You're very precious to me." Slog leaned in to the caress as a pet might do its owner.

"I hope you understand that. I'm only trying to correct you. You understand that, don't you? This is necessary." He placed his hand over Slog's chest and then turned away.

"Now, where did we leave off?" The Maker sat down in a chair beside the bed and began reading aloud from the same book of fables he read from a thousand times before. The same book Slog read to me. I turned to leave and felt a malicious presence in the dark. A shadow belonging to no one. It was shapeless, a looping cloud of black filaments. And just as it appeared, it was gone.

I moved on but continued my secret visits to

the infirmary. The airy spaces, the wide windows, the long curtains separating empty beds. I would watch The Maker tinker with Slog, twisting coils of copper, replacing patches of skin, and oiling gears and cogs within his rotten innards. He'd wind Slog's mechanical brain like a clock. I remain confused by My Maker's opposing natures. And whispering his tiny vents of black vapor into his lips. Perhaps punishing him and rewarding him was a method of mind control. Or perhaps the Maker was a slave to his own madness. I wish I knew more about him, but it wasn't meant to be. I couldn't bear that place any longer. I began to plan my emancipation. At night, I would search the fortress looking for the things I would need. I found his treasury and took three chests of gold and a bag of jewels and hid them in the stables.

One night, I found my way into the cellars. The stench was overwhelming. Filth, rotten things, death. Empty cages lined the dimly lit catacombs. I walked slowly down the rows. Each cage was covered in feculent hay and old chunks of meat rotting in stained troughs. On the back of the stone walls there were markings, some looked like an attempt at language, others were lines of time, or seemed to be, marking the days and months they were kept captive here. I felt dizzy. These were my, in some sinister way, my brothers. I could easily end up charred in the furnace as they did.

I turned to leave when I heard a faint, I don't know what it was, a whimper perhaps, coming from the far corner. I made my way quietly over to it and there, in one of the cages, was another, a half-man, similar to me. Same height, same skin tone, same symbols marked his body. Outside of the cage was a sign that read SPECIMAN BA'AL. He was starving to death. He had been forgotten. He rolled to his knees and grabbed the bars and moaned hideously. Long dirty hair covered his face. His hands were filthy and his nails were long and jagged. I could see his trough was empty, no water in sight. I felt pity for him. I rummaged around quickly, still mindful not to get caught in this dreadful place, and found a canter of water. I tossed it to him through the bars and he lifted above his head and let the water pour into his mouth and down his face. He looked to me with what I discerned as gratitude. I could see him now. I was a bit startled by the third eye just above his eyebrows. It was milky white and I assumed it was blind. Slog would later explain that it was for seeing in the dark. But let's not digress. He slowly extended his arm through the bars as if asking for more – food or water – probably both. I couldn't risk being down there any longer. I turned to leave and he fell back into the rotting hay and began to sob like a child. I stopped. I couldn't leave him. The furnace was better than starving alone in the dark. I broke the lock with ease and lifted him to a standing position. I placed one arm beneath his arms and he wrapped his boney arms around my shoulders. He grunted something that sounded like appreciation and we started moving slowly down the hall toward the furnace chamber. I kept thinking the Maker would find us, that we would turn a corner and there he'd be, fire in his eyes and we'd both be kindling. But we kept moving. Faster and faster. Poor Ba'al's legs were too weak and I was basically carrying him down the dark rows of empty cages. I was so worried about being caught I didn't notice Ba'al had begun sniffing my hair and neck. I didn't notice the drool that began to drip from his lips, or the way he suddenly tightened his grip around my neck. We were just about to reach the furnace chamber when he attacked me. Ba'al dug his jagged nails into my shoulders and chest and opened his mouth wide. I could see three rows of square teeth just before he began biting at me like a wild animal. I easily lifted him into the air and hurled him down the row of cells. He stood quickly with hunger in his heart, raced at me with a speed I assumed impossible by a creature in his condition. He lunged at me and I throw a single, powerful punch into his gaping mouth that shattered his face and sent his lower jaw spinning into the air. He fell flat on his back and began kicking at me. His toenails were like talons. I snapped his shin and dropped over him. I landed three more blows to his head and neck, destroying what was left of his face, until he finally stopped moving. From the gaping maw of his mouth a thin line of black vapor billowed up and vanished. My brother, indeed. I understood now what Slog meant about these half-men and why I was so special to the Maker. I grabbed Ba'al's broken wrist and began dragging him back to his cell.

Down the corridor, I saw movement. A shape. Not human. As if the darkness had come alive and formed itself into a, I don't know really, a haze, a mist, a shifting loop of liquid black filaments. I stopped and gazed at it. I felt my soul freeze over. I remembered the story my Maker told me about the black vapor that left his lungs after Magus resurrected him. I remembered thinking that something very evil had been unleashed into the world and this evil was searching for something very specific. It didn't seem interested in Ba'al or me, it seemed, it's hard to describe how or why I discerned this, but it seemed to be learning, it seemed to be searching. For what or whom I do not know. But as it quick as it appeared, it disappeared just the same.

I left Ba'al's broken body in his cell and made my way back to my chamber.

I found Slog among his beloved books, sitting with his back to me. The smell of charred meat filled the room. He turned and looked at me gently with those inky black eyes and smiled. He was eating an arm.

"Oh, don't let this upset you, Cronus," he said, "no need to let them go to waste in the furnace."

He was changing. His flesh was rotting at the edges, turning hard and flies buzzed around him. Was he dying? I'm not sure if it was simply my eyes playing tricks or if every time he spoke a wisp of black smog slipped from his lips. But I couldn't think about this now. I begged him to come with me. He smiled and shook his head, "This is where I belong. With the Maker. The world will see me as a monster. This is my home. It's our home. One day you will realize this too and will return to us." He wrapped his long spidery hands around mine and said, "I will miss you my brother. You have been so kind to me, Cronus. So kind."

Again, I begged him to come but he remained unmoved. "I cannot. He'd never allow it. I'm a disappointment to him. Just look at me. I'm falling to pieces. But you, well, you're perfect," he smiled, "And I knew this day would come. Your libertine spirit is what makes you so special. I've arranged a transport ship at the docks. Say my name and they will take you anywhere you desire. Anywhere in the world. I've prepared some supplies for you. I tailored a few garments for you to wear. You can't go into the world wearing only a loin cloth, my friend." He chuckled.

Lightning struck outside. A storm was coming. "You should go now. The storm will keep most ships off the water but our captain has been paid well enough to take you as ordered. Just promise me you will return someday."

I hesitated but said, "I promise."

And with a quick embrace, his body was soft like rotten meat, and I raced to the stables to get the gold and silver and made my way to the docks. Slog had done well. I found his pirate captain and he did as commanded. We set out into the thundering waves and screaming storm. I kept looking back, expecting the Maker to appear on deck in a blast of purple smoke or down below in my chamber but he didn't.

So, without boring you too much I will keep the details to a minimum. I traveled the world and explored strange lands. Tropical islands where women painted themselves in emerald symbols and built mighty pyramids in honor of their goddess Arith. We spent a month there learning their magic and alchemy and their exceptional knowledge of architecture. We sailed the seas again and visited many ports, fought pirates and sea monsters. Landed on a rocky atoll inhabited by cannibal giants. We stole their massive weapons and burned their huts in the night. For days we could hear their roars in the distance. Luckily, they couldn't swim.

After six months I was weary of the ocean wanted to be back on land. We found port in a kingdom called Ruk. A barbaric place filled with scoundrels and thieves. It was perfect for my needs. I hired the best mercenaries to train me for battle; I wore the finest clothes and purchased the most talented concubines. After a time I left Ruk and joined a mercenary force. We fought in many wars. Slaughtered men, women, and children for untold riches. And wine, yes, always the wine. I was cruel, reckless and wild.

Now, you may wonder why I have, after all these years, ages and ages, yes, deep waterfalls of time, chosen to reveal myself. I could tell you that I no longer thunder at the endless sky, that the hate has left me, dissolved in a molecular mist, that I'm more likely to find kinship in these dwindling candles than the flame that burns them. Yes, I could tell you that there is no joy to be found in the new death I've poured over the world. That I've lost everything that ever meant anything to me. That I am a failure. And it would be true. But it is also the anchors of love that have brought me to this moment. And honestly, I can't endure the secrets any longer.

Throughout my existence, I have known unimagined pleasure and boundless wealth. I have known emptiness and loneliness beyond description. I have persisted beyond the rise and fall of some of the greatest empires ever conceived. I squandered away centuries like a petty gambler losing coins in a back-alley dice game. I once spent an entire year in the golden brothel of Tologas, whose pleasure palace spans a mountaintop, without once leaving the titanic bed of its nine painted mistresses. Half a century later I would sit in a moldy cave for three years, wearing nothing but animal pelts, memorizing *The Adamic Book of the Dead,* and since I do not need to eat or drink for survival (I can and do enjoy it but it's unnecessary), I had a much easier time than the monk who accompanied me. I have splurged, recklessly, the minutes and moments that you treasure. I have butchered armies of men into mountains of bloody debris. I have sent entire races into extinction. Beautiful species of humans wiped away by my arrogance and wrath. Yet none of this satiated my longing. Life had become dull and disappointing.

After years of excess I returned to my Maker's mountaintop castle to take refuge in education. It had been almost a century since we last saw each other, but he barely raised an eyebrow at my return. He inspected me as if I was livestock. He tugged at my skin and pinched my shoulders, opened my mouth and examined my teeth, made me undress to inspect the rest of me. I learned early not to interrupt and to ignore the humiliation. He spoke as he took notes, "No regression, no decay, muscle development, reflexes, all superior." Our eyes met only briefly but it was still within the confines of examination. He told me to look right then left. The veins in the eyes, I later learned, determine the amount of this magic soul vapor that inhabits a being. He was satisfied and moved on. He searched for any defect, a scar, a bruise, a cataract or broken blood vessel, nothing. He lowered his head to his notes and asked, "Do you still speak?"

"Yes."

"What is your name?"

"Cronus Five, fifth of my name."

"And do you know who I am?"

"You're my Maker."

"And what I have I done?"

"You've made man."

Delighted, he marched away to his private study, never glancing up from the notes, and locked the massive door behind him. I was home. And then I heard a familiar clicking. I turned to see Slog. He smiled a big copper smile and said, "Welcome home, brother." He was worse off than before. New stitches here and there, a few new patches of flesh stapled to the back of skull. His body was breaking down and parts of him seemed to dissolve away in a black ash as he moved. We embraced and I said, "It's good to see you." His black eyes were wet with joy. Ignatius scurried over and hugged my knee. He whistled a beautifully happy melody. I patted him on the head and stroked his small patch of red hair that capped his little bald head and said, "It's so good to be home brothers."

Slog grinned, "Would you care for some wine? I've been saving some for your return."

"Later," I said. "I want to see the library."

"Oh, there'll be time for books later. Let's celebrate."

"I've been drinking for a century. I need to dry up."

"Oh, come now. You must listen to me. Out of we three brothers, I am the oldest."

"Yes," I smiled and stood tall, "but I'm the biggest. Slog smiled.

"Ignatius can take you. It's too dark for me." Ignatius whistled a melody and clapped quietly. I smiled and said, "Lead the way, brother."

And so it was we entered the vast catacombs of the library with Ignatius illuminating the way. My Maker, the immortal, the genius – his library rivaled the great one at Alexandria. I stayed there for months and studied endlessly. There were times I felt that ominous presence in the dark. That looping, gelatinous shadow watching from the dark. But I paid no mind to it. Some nights, through the thick walls, I could hear vague sounds of music and dancing, but mostly it was silent. Then, as I was reading a book of botany scribed by the monks of Coalhar when I heard a terrifying screech in one of the dark catacombs. I thought I saw a flash of Ignatius, his golden light flashing frightfully in the dark, before being absorbed into shadow. I searched and searched but Ignatius was nowhere to be found. I asked Slog about it and he dismissed me immediately claiming that Ignatius has a habit of disappearing. There was something wrong about his story. I couldn't determine what it was but he was definitely holding something back. Then, as if picking up on my disbelief said that perhaps the Maker had sent him away. At night, in distorted dreams, I saw poor Ignatius, beautiful as he was, being devoured by that strange shadowy

Thing that haunted the catacombs.

I returned to the library and continued my studies. One day Slog came to me and insisted I get some fresh air. Reluctantly I agreed and walked down into the surrounding village. Summer was upon us. I remember walking down the knobby earth, through the ramshackle village of rock and mud huts and tented markets to a frenzied scene. Today, a caravan was in from the north and with it came money and supplies to be traded. The winding streets bustled with energy. People crowded the walkways begging for food. Fathers offered their children to the brothels in hopes of gold or spices. It was common to see a man dragging his young child, male or female, kicking and screaming to the purple tents of the flesh peddlers. Normally, I would pass by without a single glance. What should I care if the animals bred? Or fed? But as I made my way through the people, towering above them in my black robes, my eyes met those of a small child, barely six years of age. One of her eyes was swollen shut, her lip creased with dried blood. Her ivory limbs, slender from hunger, were ruined with bruises. Something happened to me at that moment. I am no poet, I do not possess the heart of a romantic, but I swear to you that she looked into my soul and I into hers. The spell lasted briefly before her father, a brick of a man who smelled distinctly of manure and sour wine, snatched her by her tiny wrist and dragged her into one of the purple tents. He made a deal with the perfumed mistress and placed his daughter on the bed. The mistress's body bulged between the folds of linen that wrapped her. She nodded in agreement and exited the tent for another.

A line of men, ten or so, waited outside, passing a bottle back and forth and laughing about what each hoped to do the girl. I moved closer, unsure of what I intended to do. I could hear the girl whimpering, calling out for a mother lost in the grave, as her father ordered her to remain calm.

"Be still, girl. They will be done quicker if you don't fight."

One of the men called out, "Don't take all the spirit out of her!" The others laughed drunkenly. The largest of the men pushed forward; he'd had enough. An old scar dissected his face. His filthy cloaks were that of a mercenary. He choked back a bottle of sour wine, tossed it aside, and handed the father a single coin. The large man entered the tent. I could hear the girl crying louder as he prepared to mount her. Her screams carried down the length of the village, joined the bartering voices and wooden flutes of the serpent dancers, and became part of the common chorus. The father eyed the bottle of sour wine still passing between the men, the craving eating at his features. He walked to each man, taking coins one by one, licking his dried lips with the tip of his froggish tongue.

A young pock-faced man resisted, "What if she dies before I get my turn? I'm not giving up the gold yet." An older one leaned forward, sloppy from wine, and pressed a dirty coin into the father's hand. "It doesn't matter to me."

When her cries of terror turned into screams of pain, I was moving at them before I realized it. Maybe it was the bottles of sour wine that gave them drunken courage, but they stepped up. They assumed I was trying to skip ahead of them. They were wrong. Wrath washed over my mind and in a moment I knew exactly how I was going to dispatch this rotten crew.

Her father lunged at me and I sent my fist into his jaw with such speed and power that his head spun round and met his backbone. I front kicked the next one, crushing his heart and lungs, and his ribcage ruptured out of his sides like the wings of a dead bird. He tumbled into the one directly behind him as I drew my sword and lopped off the heads of three men and opened the throats of two more. I gutted the fat one who ran at me with a shovel, sliced another completely in half with a vertical swing of my sword, and then spun around to send my blade into the heart of the man running up behind me. This all happened in a matter of seconds before the man in the tent left the girl and was rushing to see what was happening. Before he could draw his sword, his gut met my blade. I opened him up, and reached inside the gash, pushed past his intestines, my iron gloves cutting the soft organs, and gripped his heart. He was strong and tried to fight, but he was no match for me. I pulled him close, stared into his inferior eyes and plucked his heart like a fig. I stepped over his crumpled body into the tent. The girl was tiny. She scrambled away from me, gripping her knees to her chest and crossing her feet. I picked her up slowly and carried her from that awful place. She was filthy, and her tattered clothing was held together by threads. As I marched through the village, the crowds parted and averted their gaze. As soon as we had left the border and I made my way up the steep incline to the castle, the voices and music rose slowly behind me. I carried her up with such care that she fell asleep in my arms. I placed her in one of the receiving rooms and beseeched Slog for help.

"Please watch her for a moment." Slog nodded and hastened to the girl.

"We should call-call-call," he stuttered, "for

the witch."

"Do it. I'll alert the Maker."

I made my way down the long, dim hallway to my Maker's study. He sat, as he always did, at the center of a long table. Overspread with quills and ink wells, candles and oil lamps, glass tubes that transported bubbling liquids of all colors to heated beakers, scrolls were tossed wildly and piled over uneaten plates of moldy food. His nose pointed in the center of a dusty tome feverishly taking notes. I stood in the doorway and dared not enter without an invitation.

"Maker?" He didn't look up. The corner of his mouth twitched on one side.

"What is it?"

"Sir, I've taken a ...ward. A child. She's injured. May I call the witch?"

He ran his hand through his black and silver hair. The thick curls bounced back and took the shape of a stormy sea.

"The midwife?"

"Yes. The midwife."

"Fine. I'm expecting a batch of her elixirs from her. Once she's done with the child, bring the bottles to me."

"As you wish." I slipped into the darkened hallway and returned to the room. Slog had already sent a rider to retrieve the witch, excuse me, the midwife. As we waited, we did what we could for the child. After a time we heard the clatter of hooves returning and Slog slipped off through a hidden passage in the wall. No one was to ever see him or Ignatius. I ran to the entrance and let her in. She was not what I expected. This was no crone. She wasn't hook-nosed or covered in boils or spiders. She was young and beautiful, with dark flowing hair and green eyes. I think I fell in love with her on the spot. She said, "My name's Elsbeth. Master Thoth sent for me." (Master Thoth – so subtle – was one of my Maker's many aliases.)

I probably stared longer than I realized because she said, "Are you the one that needs my assistance?" I snapped out of it and led her to the girl. I explained what happened and she said, "You're very kind. Most girls like her end up as food for feral dogs."

I averted my gaze as Elsbeth examined the poor little creature.

"She's still …intact," Elsbeth said with grace. "And aside from a few cuts and bruises, she's fine. She just needs a warm meal, a warm bath, and comfortable bed."

"My Ma--," I caught myself. "I mean, Master Thoth appreciates your help and asks if you know a safe place for her?"

"Yes," said Elsbeth, rubbing ointment on the

girl's wounds, "there's an abbey just beyond the Silver Forest. If your rider will be so kind, I can take her."

"I'll arrange for transport immediately. Thank you, Elsbeth." I handed her a small bag of coins.

"It's my sacred duty," she said, placing the bag in her cloak. "I didn't get your name."

"Cronus."

"Such a unique name," she smiled. "Well, give my regards to Master Thoth. Oh, and these." She handed me a consignment of little bottles. "Tell him I'll have another batch by the next full moon."

"I will."

"Thank you, Cronus."

We stood staring for a few moments and then I led her to the entrance. I placed the child in the carriage and told the driver to be swift. Elsbeth smiled and they rode away.

Now, dear reader, I have known true love but once in my long life. Elsbeth. I grew to love her, to admire her, to need her. I went back to her to get an update on the girl. She was fine I was told. Then, our eyes met again and our courtship began. I won't bore you with the sentimental details, it's not that kind of story, but I admit it was magical. We grew to love each other. I stayed the same but she blossomed into a beautiful woman. We were inseparable. She loved the castle, she loved Slog, she loved me. It was my first time knowing true, unconditional love. I was hers forever.

Our first night as lovers was our wedding night – as was the custom. We would soon learn, however, that I am unable to father children. Whether or this deficiency is deliberate or not, I will never know. But so it is. We were married in the great chamber of my birth. The slab served as the altar and Slog performed the ceremony by moonlight. My Maker gave us the east wing of the castle to live in. I'm not sure why he was so generous; I took his offer without asking. And so it was for a time that we lived in blissful innocence. I suppose it was the newness of love that kept me from the realization that one-day she would grow old, and I would not. That she would get sick, and I would not. That one day I would be putting her body in the ground, and I would be alone again. But then she fell ill with fever. And it was love that fueled the flame that warmed my soul. I refused to be cold again. I set about trying to decipher my Maker's work and adapt it for my own. I needed to make her immortal. My Maker's genius was too great. I couldn't understand his research. So I looked to the library.

(Note: you may find all this research in the accompanying notes; however, I have encrypted it so that only men of some intellectual means can access it. I've done enough damage. This is a safety measure.)

I found a row of clay jars each marked with a single hieroglyph. The largest jar held a group of papyrus written by a mysterious alchemist named ehd-Qurom. The title of the work was *Endless Dawn.* Imprinted on the scrolls were detailed instructions on the preparation of a body for immortality through the use a very rare fungus. It took some doing to extract a living specimen. The fungal spores invade a living host through the airways, lodging and ultimately growing inside the brain along the nerve path. In an effort to extend its own life, the fungus encourages cell repair and thus fends off sickness and aging. I flipped through the papyrus, reading as fast as I could, digesting the data, page after page of unbelievable fortune! The last papyrus had been burned at the bottom. I could make out but a few passages. One warned that the fungus also stimulates the metabolism so much so that hunger was unmanageable for some subjects to the point where a few ate (something missing) in their sleep. Another passage stated very clearly that the fungus wouldn't regenerate limbs or give youth to the old. Though it does improve strength and focus, it only stops death and sickness from progressing at the point it invades the subject. So if a blind man were infected, he would live forever a blind man. The final passage trailed off into the segment charred by fire. The rest of the scroll included several final steps necessary to complete the process but most was missing in the burned area. I was confident I could discover the final instructions either in another scroll or perhaps in my Maker's research, or by my own ingenuity.

I did not.

By the time I realized I might never discover the secret, Elsbeth's illness had worsened. She was barely thirty years old and had contracted the fever that vanquished the surrounding village. Now it had come to the high castle walls. My Maker was off on one of his expeditions, and he had taken Slog and Ignatius with him. I was forced to go it alone. I hired servants to maintain the castle and guards to patrol the grounds. I didn't want to be disturbed.

The instructions stated (and I'm leaving out a few for security) that after procuring the herbs, vines, and fungi, they were to be dried, ground with blood, heated to a boil and left to cool for half a day. This allowed the tiny spores to pop from their protective buds and wait for pollination. Then, by moonlight, the mixture was to be broken down into a fine dry powder. Blood red and charcoal black, the powder was to be blown into the nostrils. The converted would then experience a deep euphoria before falling limp, allowing the spores to travel up the nostrils, to the thin membrane that houses the brain, and take root.

A side note, I've relocated from my writing desk to a table closer to the arrowslit to capture a bit of moonlight. The candles are waning over the stacks of books and scrolls and the many crates of explosives I have placed near the sealed entrance, and it's becoming ever more difficult to write. Perhaps it's the wine, but as I peer through the window, I spy a purple comet streaking through the sky. Perhaps it's Magus returning to reclaim what he gave my Maker. Maybe he can lead me to him. Maybe I'll escape using one of Slog's hidden doorways. Maybe I'll find Magus, I'll find my Maker, and I'll right this wrong. Maybe.

I've had to stop writing several times now in order to refortify the door. My children are strong and hungry, but I'm not ready for them yet. From the distant choruses rising all around me, it seems we haven't much time before they congest the cavern and the bombs detonate. As much as it pains me to admit, as much horror as it brings to write this, I'm very proud of them. They never cease to amaze me with their evolving abilities. Just a year ago, it would have taken them three times as long to scour the neck of the escarpment and sniff me out. But I must put away my foolish pride and have this finished and tossed from the arrowslit or else lose the chance I so desperately want to explain myself to you and hopefully assist in ending this menace.

Elsbeth had slipped into a coma. The fever was progressing. I acted quickly, blindly, without thinking. I followed the formula. I ground the fungus; I mixed it with my own blood, and baked it in the fire. I crushed it into a powder and used a small tube to blow the black powder into her nostrils. For a moment, nothing, and then she sat up screaming and rubbing her face as if it were on fire. She thrashed on the bed like a wild animal. I tried to stop her but she fell to the floor with a sickening thump. I thought she broke her neck. I turned her over. She was already progressing into the euphoric phase. Her eyes floated in her skull, and a slow smile cut across her face. She slipped back into unconsciousness. I lifted her to the bed and covered her with a blanket. An hour had gone by. I noticed she stopped breathing. I shook her. She was dead. I called for a guard to watch the room. I ran to my Maker's study. Slog begged me to stop. He did. "You're not thinking clearly, Cronus. Listen to me my brother. She's gone. Whatever else you do will be an abomination. I've seen this before. You must stop. Besides, the Maker will not allow this and you will have done something you cannot undo."

But I wouldn't listen. He grabbed my arm and said, "Please brother, stop." But I shoved him down the corridor. His arm broke in three places, a large portion of his leg dissolved to black ash. He looked at me with such pain and betrayal. I felt sorry for what I had done but all I could think of was Elsbeth. I had to get to my Maker's study. Slog drug himself down the passage and that was the last I saw of him. I ran faster and faster. Perhaps there was a book or a scroll, something that I missed. But as soon as I reached the door a terrifying scream echoed through the entire castle. I raced back to Elsbeth. I found her in the corridor, straddling the lifeless body of the guard, eating his face. I pulled her off and she went after me. Clawing and biting. I wrapped her in my cloak and called for the guards to bring me heavy chains.

"My darling, what have I done?"

The guards came with shackles and we carried her to room where I was born. We fastened her to the wall. I locked the door and left her there.

My apologies, dear reader, but I need a moment to compose myself. Perhaps more wine will help. Wine always helps.

After chaining her inside the chamber, I

thought to defang her but couldn't bring myself to do it. So I had the blacksmith forge a special helmet that restricted her biting but allowed me to see her face. It didn't go well. Without the ability to feed, decomposition is rapid. Flies gathered beneath the iron hood and laid their pearly eggs. It was horrendous. We removed it, and I sought a surgical remedy. I tried removing just her jaw at first, so she couldn't bite, but this only led to frenzy. Her tongue jutted out like a green worm. The thick pus dripping from her open throat dribbled like rancid honey over her beautiful gown. I searched for a cure, working tirelessly in my laboratory. I applied all varieties of salves and powders, potions and even magic spells, but nothing worked. Her body grew cold. Gone were the fevers and hallucinations. What was left was putrid. A creature piggishly grunting, moaning and screeching with hunger. I ordered slabs of raw meat fresh from the butcher's blade dropped at her feet, but it was of no interest to her. Those green eyes that once stared into mine on long nights by firelight were now white as a spider's egg. Those eyes, dead but alive, with their reptilian stare, searched only for movement. Her nose sniffed the air for living prey as her rancid body rocked back and forth at the length of the chain.

My beloved Elsbeth, once beautiful and

true, now a rancid thing propelled by hellish hunger.

I had to remove the tips of her fingers; the nails, as you know, are quite dangerous. I caught her just after she seized another guard. She had hacked him to pieces with her talons. She was hunched over his macerated flesh, using her tongue and upper jaw, sucking at the open gashes like a fly. After her fingertips were removed, she used the moldy nubs of her broken fingers to open a servant's throat. She was able to stuff several large pieces of meat down the hole where her mouth once was, but the mass lodged inside the tube of her throat and stayed there to rot. The smell was difficult for the servants and guards. They burned incense and saturated the chamber with fresh flowers. I imported perfume, but it only decorated the odor. And the windows had to remain sealed. I couldn't chance the possibility of her escaping.

I know what you're thinking, and it's true, but I was selfish. I couldn't let her go. I was hoping my Maker would return and help me reverse this. But he didn't come. And I went mad. I tried correcting the formula. I had my guards kidnap drunkards and I'd feed them the powder. They would turn, as my Elsbeth did, into ghouls. My children. That's what they are to me. I know, insanity. I tried again and again, infecting drunkards, orphans, and prostitutes, those who would not be missed, infecting them with this evil. The cells in the dungeon were filled with my monstrous children.

Meanwhile, I ordered my men to bind Elsbeth's arms to her sides, but the chain knifed into her moldy flesh and looked as if it would dissect her. So we placed her inside a special iron cabinet resembling a standing sarcophagus. Normally used for torture, it would provide a means to keep her safe and in one piece. The shape of the sarcophagus was carefully crafted to resemble Elsbeth, with a cast likeness of her face. In the end, I intended it to be her tomb, but I couldn't bring myself to bury her this way. Screaming for eternity beneath the cold earth inside this iron box.

Madness was growing inside the castle. The guards began refusing to enter her chamber. I wouldn't accept this sort of insurrection, so they found another way to serve me: in the dungeon, as food for the children.

As the days passed and nights grew longer, her screams became louder and more desperate. Opening the double doors of the sarcophagus revealed the chains had almost cut her in two. Black blood bubbled down her body like fresh tar. Her bones were protruding through the broken skin. It had to stop. I ordered my guards to drag the sarcophagus to the courtyard and build a bonfire. I heated my sword until it glowed white-hot and with two quick strikes removed her arms. My guards tossed her arms into the fire. I've learned to destroy all remnants of them once they have been converted. A single finger of a convert can reanimate and pollinate its evil seed into another. A scratch, a bite, any method of entering the bloodstream will work.

I could tell from the way she stood, crooked, almost adjacent to her legs, that the lack of feeding was taking its toll. The rotting was rapid and ever increasing. Her spine had broken, her legs had dislodged, and if not for the sack of skin holding her together, her bones would have spilled over the floor. I raised my mighty sword once more and in a single swipe cut her clean through, sending her lower parts flailing across the room. I was delirious. I thought I was helping but this only led to a more hideous version of her. This was no longer my Elsbeth. I sent my men to the armaments to retrieve my dress armor and weapons of adornment.

So it was, on a cold night just over a century ago that I butchered my precious wife with the battle-axe I plucked a hundred years before from the dead grip of the savage king of Chlandia and burned her beneath the winter moon. And as the ashes fell to the bloody earth, I found myself overwhelmed. For the first time in my long burdensome life I wished for death.

Forgive me. I have stopped writing again and finished another canter of wine because the sound of my children has grown. The door is giving way. I suppose I shouldn't have wasted your time with the last part. It isn't true. The reason I call them my children is because Elsbeth and I created them. You see, in the beginning, after she, well, converted, I wasn't aware that if she only ate half the body, the remaining bits would reanimate and convert. I didn't know that once converted they too had the power to convert their food into Eaters. And this is how the world died. And this is why I lied. And now the door is breaking. And now they are clawing over each other to get inside. And they are coming. Elsbeth is with them. And I wait for her to give me one last kiss. I must write more quickly. It's almost over now. There was a kind of romance in the madness. We were creating children together. Monsters though they were, they belonged to us. We would wander the countryside, I leading her by a chain, and we would hunt together. Once fed, I placed her back in her sarcophagus, and I slept by firelight.

This continued for three years, and as she ate, the rotting slowed. I had it in my head that if she ate enough she might someday be restored. But my madness dissipated when Elsbeth escaped her sarcophagus and made her way through the Silver Forest to an abbey. By the time I found Elsbeth, the nuns, the orphans, all of them, were half eaten and now converted into Eaters. The grim reality punched the breath out of me. My sword was swift. I butchered them. I trapped Elsbeth and dragged her back to the castle. I placed her in the sarcophagus and sunk her in the swamp behind the gardens. For the next hundred years, I hunted my children. I found them where they nested, and I cut them down. I traveled the world trying to end what I began, but their illness mutated and spread rapidly. Rumors came to me of a shadowy form walking the ancient grounds of my home. I returned hoping it was my Maker, but it was Elsbeth. Walking slowly through the grounds, searching for food, a strange looping shadow following her. A shadow that wasn't hers. She had escaped from the swamp. And now she's here, in front of me. Her rotten skull is moaning through the door. Her steps are slow. Her bones are old and moldy. The barricade is holding but not for much longer. For a moment, I thought I heard the old familiar sound of clicking and gears turning. Could it be? Has my brother Slog returned? In the shadows of the far corner I swear I could see two eyes, black as oil, with two tiny pinpricks of light staring at me. But the form is shapeless, a looping circle of black filaments, as if the darkness had come alive.

Oh, how I wish I could see my brothers to say goodbye. How I wish I could see my Maker again and feed him to my children. But it's too late. I have yet to decide if I will offer myself to my children. I don't even know if that will work. I doubt their teeth could break my skin. So do I exterminate myself, my children and this castle with explosives or do I escape and bury them in rubble? I can't decide. Perhaps wine will help. Wine always helps.

As I sit here on top of the world all I see is emptiness. I know there is no cure. There will never be a cure. There is no cure for hunger or greed or selfishness. There is no cure for any of us.

We are the disease.

Thank you dear reader for allowing me once again inside your infinite minds. It means everything to me.

Love & Stitches,
Otep

Otep Shamaya is an author, songwriter, artist, activist, a GLAAD nominee, cultural arsonist, BAFTA award winner, MTV Music Award winner & last true mouthpiece with a fearless passion for justice and the preservation of the arts. This is her first book of short stories.

LIVE TO DEFY.

Centaurs Breed Publishing

Also by Otep Shamaya:

- None Shall Sleep
- Caught Screaming
- Quiet Lightning on the Noisy Mountain
- New Word Order
- The Myth
- The Sugar Shack

Find them online at:
www.lulu.com/spotlight/otepsaves

Find Otep Shamaya online at:

- www.instagram.com/otepofficial
- www.facebook.com/otepofficial
- www.twitter.com/otepoffical

MOVIES IN MY HEAD

BY OTEP SHAMAYA

Centaurs Breed Publishing

For information about this publication contact: **girlgoesgrrr@gmail.com**